More Critical Praise for Daniel Buckman's *Water in Darkness*:

"Simply put, *Water in Darkness* is a superb novel, a tasty piece of storytelling. Daniel Buckman's tale is a roller coaster ride, told from that blunt, dark place where the rubber meets the road ... Here is an earthbound 'Chicago' style that harkens back to *Studs Lonigan*, and reminds one of the close-to-the-bone, walk-the-plank stories of Mike Royko, Stuart Dybek, and Nelson Algren. Buckman speaks for a new, young generation of soldiers who thought they were at peace. *Water in Darkness* is a sterling piece of work—the best new fiction I have read in a good long while."
–Larry Heinemann, author of *Paco's Story*, winner of the National Book Award

"Daniel Buckman has that power that few writers have, not just to describe but to really make us feel the pain and the joy of this extraordinary life in human flesh. *Water in Darkness* is not just a book about soldiers, it's a book about what happens to human weakness when it's forced inside a uniform, forced to be strong, forced to live with hurt and loss. This book puts Buckman up there with the big names already." –Gerry Nicosia, author of *Home to War*

"Just when you think it is safe to forget about the Vietnam War, something forces it back into consciousness. Perhaps it is former Nebraska Senator Bob Kerrey's nightmare of having to relive, live on CNN, the horror of a night thirty years ago in the Mekong Delta. Perhaps it is a book like Daniel Buckman's *Water in Darkness*." –*Los Angeles Times*

"Daniel Buckman conjures up scenes reminiscent and worthy of Nelson Algren himself. Like Algren, Buckman obviously knows Chicago's dark crevices and seedy history well ... Some characters ooze with the evil they have become from the hand life has dealt them. Others are seeking and worthy of redemption, yet seem resigned to an eternity chained to their internal and external demons." –*Hartford Courant*

"*Water in Darkness* is a wonderful novel ... I eagerly anticipate Buckman's next work." –BookBrowser.com

"... an assured debut novel ... a gritty tale rendered with tough, spare prose that fits the story like a flak jacket." –Popmatters.com

THE NAMES *of* RIVERS

DANIEL BUCKMAN

AKASHIC BOOKS

NEW YORK

The author wishes to acknowledge his debt of gratitude to Ronald Regner, Robert Otvos, Leo Baglarz, and Katherine Drayne Blount, his editor.

This is a work of fiction. All names, characters, places, and incidents are the product of the author's imagination. Any resemblance to real events or persons, living or dead, is entirely coincidental.

Published by Akashic Books
©2002 Daniel Buckman

Cover photo by
ISBN: 1-888451-29-7
Library of Congress Control Number: 2002101543

First printing

Akashic Books
PO Box 1456
New York, NY 10009
Akashic7@aol.com
www.akashicbooks.com
Printed in Canada

For Gerald C. Buckman and George L. Pomon Jr.

The three flannel shirts the old man wore for a coat barely warmed him against the wind gusting in from the fields. He pitched the cigar butt aside and dropped the pickup gate and set the chain to keep it flat. The dogs jumped up with lolling tongues and leaned their muddy paws on the gate to see. The motorbike frame was rusted and lying across the bed, its engine stripped down to gummy parts inside a cardboard box. The old man bid three times for this 1926 Whizzer at an estate auction near Chebanse where men in plaid mackinaws milled beneath the awning on the farmhouse lawn, picking among the dead man's tools strewn on metal tables. They waved and nodded bids while the red-faced auctioneer ranted into a bullhorn and fought to keep his shirt tucked in around his stomach. The widow looked on from the porch and cried into a wadded tissue. She was flanked by two fat women he took to be her church friends.

Her knees buckled and the women carried her back into the house and drew the curtains.

The dogs howled and jumped from the truck bed but stayed close, rearing and barking as if bound by a leash. The old man turned to look when a young buck came walking out of the trees behind his tiny clapboard house. He met the buck's eyes and the dogs went silent. He raised his hand and the deer went back upon muddy haunches and flailed its forelegs before turning and bounding off into the flooded fields.

"Son of a bitch," he said. "Goddamn son of a bitch."

He saw this deer forty years ago in the last days of the war in Europe when lightning came stranger than he'd ever known, the bolts circling the sky like the coiling of a rope. The buck loped from the beech trees and ran across spring grass scarred by retreating Panzer columns. Dachau rose upon a hillside, but what it was his squad had three hundred yards to know. He was a sergeant of infantry back then, and the lung blood of Bobby Wilburn stained his jacket sleeve. Wilburn got killed by a sniper after stand-to. The dumb hayshaker was like a cat, always having to shit alone where the world was quiet. He led his squad ahead of the Sherman tanks, off across the muddy grass until the diesel engines became mute, then fanned out into an uneven rank without sunlight above to lay down their shadows. The buck ran within a rifle's length of the soldiers, fuming cold breath from its nose. They called to it. Some whistled. The buck looked at him while passing and disappeared over a hill. He felt strangely alone like the deer was a guide deserting him, his way back now lost forever.

The barbed wire fence dripped rain while the gray faces looked at them as if embarrassed. The starved men were all clones. They mimicked the act of eating and murmured different languages. Some shoved hands through the wire that were not hands but claws. He and his squad only looked back, gravel-eyed beneath steel pots. They'd thought this place was a steel mill, a foundry, and the chimneys were smoke stacks. Starzack was the first to pass a chocolate bar through the wire, a Polack kid from East Chicago who before Omaha Beach was goofier than a carny barker but now was only quiet. The gray men fought and gored their arms upon the wet barbs, but the wounds were without blood. He stood back from his squad while they gave away their K-ration chocolate. The gray men hurled their bodies against the wire, but the soldiers were very careful not to touch their hands. He turned away from the bodies lying in the mud beyond the wire, their eyes open so he could not tell who was dead or alive, then looked down at Wilburn's blood, the stain made darker by the rain. A fucking corpse pile. A whole war for a goddamned corpse pile. While he raised his arm to wave down the tanks, the gray men became sick from the chocolate and collapsed. More came and took their places and grabbed through the wire for the bars.

The old man sat on the pickup gate and rolled a cigarette and lit it. The dogs were in the bed now, sniffing the box of engine parts, their fur matted from the rain. He closed his eyes without once putting the cigarette to his lips. The rain fell cold upon the deep seams of his face. He might have wanted this motorbike when he was a boy had he ever seen one and known that some boys rode down the wind. He kept his eyes closed and dreamed himself upon this Whizzer, speeding open-throttle along field roads marred by wagon wheels and sun-baked mule tracks, maybe through meadows streaked with goldenrod where cows watched him grow small in the distance.

Bruce Konick came slow through the cornfields where the stalks swayed from the first gestures of larger wind. His car rode low on its back tires, the trunk overloaded with tools. He crossed a creek and drove toward a clapboard house with a hedge of trees on both sides. Beyond it was a ruined corn-crib with the boards turned gray from the sun. He went up the gravel lane and passed a hickory tree with an engine block dangling by two chains. Five kittens drank water from an upside-down hubcap. He parked the car and walked to the house, then knocked on the storm door while a hundred blackbirds flapped south in the dusk to shut themselves of Watega County. The door opened. A man in paint-flecked coveralls spat.

"You Bruce Konick?" he said.

"Yessir."

"Andy said you'd have scars, so let's see them."

Bruce looked up and the man raised a flashlight, but he did not turn it on right away. The birds crowded a wide swath of sky. He eyed Bruce's cheek, rutted like tree bark gone blue. There was the lobeless ear that let in wind sounds even when no wind blew.

"A gook and a Chi-Com grenade did this," Bruce said. "You believe that?"

The man came down the porch steps with one leg lagging behind. Bruce saw that it was thinner by the way his pants hung loose. He moved heavily for the trunk of the car, all bent over with a hard paunch and a bony rump.

"How'd you get that chain so high in the tree?" Bruce asked. "I think you'd of needed two ladders. Nigger-rig them somehow."

The man shined the light on the trunk lock. The car was a red Pontiac with fist-sized dents across the hood. The weight bulged the tires into air tumors. The man looked at the tires, then at Bruce. He shook his head.

"Let's see what the hell you got inside this limousine," he said.

Bruce opened the trunk and inside were heaped all manner of tools. Odd wrenches and hammers and thick iron saws covered the spare. He grinned like he had something.

The man studied the tools in the flashlight's beam.

"This all you got?" he said.

"I can get more."

The man picked out a heavy saw and turned it in his hand.

"You know what the hell this is?" he said.

"They use it for thick wood. It cuts the hardest wood you can buy like it ain't nothing. I've seen them. Craftsmen."

"Craftsmen, my ass. This was for cutting ice blocks when the quarries froze over back before there was electric refrigerators. Last man that used this ain't been in business since before the war."

"Shit," Bruce said.

11

The man threw back the saw and worked the light about the other tools.

"There's a mason's chisel for scoring rock," he said. "A wrench set for a Model T Ford. Son of a bitch. You even got a hammer for shoeing a goddamn mule."

"That's a hammer for hanging trim," Bruce said. "They make them like that so the nails won't break."

"No sir," said the man. "What you got here is tools nobody needs anymore. The world don't use the shit they fix."

"They ain't that old," Bruce said. "I got everything cheap off a carpenter from Sheldon. Said he was done butchering wood and thinking about moving to Texas."

The man waved him away and shifted his weight back upon the good leg. The light lay on a well-oiled anvil, pocked from hammer hits.

"Whoever owned these tools kept them up," he said. "Like one day time is going to turn back."

"Tell me something," Bruce said.

"Forty for all of it."

"I was thinking a hundred."

"Then go on thinking."

"You wouldn't give me seventy?"

"No."

"You said they were kept up good."

The man turned off the flashlight.

"You got a wheelbarrow," Bruce said. "For five dollars more I'll unload the trunk."

"That's already figured in the forty."

"Shit."

"What do you do at General Foods?" the man said. "I know it ain't working with tools."

"I worked the machine that keeps the dog food going into the bags. Before I got laid off."

The man blew cold from his nose and let go half a laugh.

"That's perfect," he said.

* * *

The bowling alley was a long building made of cinderblocks painted white, and the neon beer signs in the
few windows blurred from the rain. Bruce looked away
from his face in the glass door and was half soaked by the
time he walked inside. A yellowish light suffused the
empty lanes where an idiot boy with swimming eyes and
tongue aloll worked a dust mop over the warped wood.
The shoe room was closed and Bruce went straight to the
bar and stood against the gummy counter of it with his
face dripping. Lorenzo the bartender looked away from a
TV full of snow, eyeing Bruce while he scratched his belly
up under his T-shirt.

"He still cost twenty dollars," Lorenzo said.

Bruce nodded and stood so he would not see himself in
the barback mirror. A pack of Winstons lay on the counter
beside an overfull ashtray.

"You play no games this time," Lorenzo said. "Twenty dollars is for one thing, forty is for another."

"I'll even get him drunk after."

"I just want to see the money."

Bruce pulled a crumpled twenty from his pocket. The
idiot boy was cleaning the lanes, laughing at nothing.

"You know twenty dollars is just for one thing," Lorenzo
said.

"I know."

"You want more, it cost more."

"I know, goddammit."

"Then no bullshit."

"I said I'll get him good and drunk after," Bruce said.

Lorenzo pocketed the money and came from behind the
bar. His back fat quivered as he walked into the pool room
where a Mexican kid stood alone shooting a cue ball across
an empty table. The brim from a straw cowboy hat was low
over his face while he stayed the cue with the stick as it spun
back. He stood straight when he saw Lorenzo and stared at
the duct tape holding together his tennis shoes. Bruce

swiped the cigarettes from the bar and walked off toward the glass doors, closing his eyes.

He sat in the car and wiped the rain from his face and lit a stolen Winston with his Third Marines Zippo. Soon the kid got inside and grinned, pushing back his hat brim. He was shy and quiet in the way of migrants who stayed in the county long after the melon harvest to work in diner kitchens amid the steam from large pots. Bruce felt the kid trying hard not to stare at his face.

"*Cerveza fría*," the kid said.

"Cold beer," Bruce said. "We'll go to that bar across the street the way Lorenzo told you in Mexican."

The kid pointed the way to the tavern. He made his fist like a can of beer and drank it down.

"Ten beers for you," Bruce said. "Ten beers for me."

He showed the kid ten fingers, then turned the ignition so the battery would juice the radio. The kid sat up like they were leaving. A mariachi song played on the AM dial, but the static from the rain made it hard to hear. Bruce snuffed his cigarette and took off the kid's hat and pitched it in the back. He slid over on the bench seat and with one hand undid his own belt. The kid let him close and ran his cold fingers up his untucked shirt tail. The rain slashed through the standing water in the gravel lot and waved the puddles while Bruce closed his eyes to the scars looking back at him in the window. Soon the night was without sound, without shadow.

It was still raining when he left the kid standing before River City Liquors with a six-pack of Busch in a paper bag. The awning sagged with water and the windows showed the headlights and the rain streaks. The wind came hard over the railroad viaduct when he backed away, blowing off the kid's hat where he stood hugging the bagged beer and staring into the rain. The hat slid across the puddles and blew into the street and off beyond the reach of the light. The kid let it go. *I might get you again. But you got to learn to keep your teeth off it. Like that boy who did it so good I wanted us to be dead together.*

14

Bruce crossed East Avenue and drove past General Foods and Roper Stove, the factories whitelit and illuminating the rain as if ships at sea. The street went curbless, empty, and unswerving along the railroad tracks, the traffic lights drooling on the glass between wiper passes. He ran a finger over his scars while he drove and felt each marring until he saw some fifteen years back into the hole at Khe Sanh *with a boy so blond and beautiful, an infant's face upon the lank body of a marine rifleman. He was asleep, wound in a muddy poncho, while the mist turned orange by dawn's light and the white birds flew over from the green hills as if retracing the way of the rockets that had struck in the night. After the attack, Bruce had loved this boy and held his face against the tightness of his stomach, but in the dawn he leaned into the back parapet of the hole with his belt undone, still feeling the wetness of the boy's lips. Bruce looked left down the perimeter; the marines facing west with their rifles for stand-to were only shadows. He held a grenade and rolled its coolness over his mouth. The boy's chest rose and fell with the breath of sleep. Bruce clasped his belt and closed his eyes before pulling the grenade pin, last hearing the fuse crack while it fell in the mud.*

The men in their stained Carhartt jackets looked up from the stools where they sat along the bar. No one looked at him very long where he stood in the waxen light of Skinny's Tap, his bangs falling long and wet across the scars. He wiped his eyes and took a stool where the counter curved into the wall, propping his boots on the rail above the tile floor. Malinda poured tequila shots for two correctional officers off their shift from the Watega County Jail. In the pale light and drifting smoke the men raised their glasses as if toasting her oriental beauty before the drink enhanced it more. They knocked back the shots and bit the limes before setting the empty glasses on the bar again. The rain spun in the street lamps outside the windows. Bruce jutted his face over the well and called her by name.

Malinda looked hard into his eyes and wrinkled her doll's

face. The correctional officers sweat along their top lips and watched her tiny backside slide around the cooler.

"You can have two beers, Bruce Konick," she said.

"I ain't drank nothing since noon."

"Two beers and you go or I call the cops."

"Shit," he said. "I know Malinda ain't your real name. You're like the guy who runs that Chinese restaurant on East Avenue. I know his name ain't Bob."

"Go to hell, Bruce Konick," she said.

Malinda set his draught down on a paper coaster.

"It's got to be Lin or Minh," Bruce said, "but your name being Malinda is like having a town in Vietnam named Watega."

"I'm Filipino, you dumb bastard."

"That ain't right about me being a bastard, Minh. I know who my old man is. It was my ma I hardly knew. Now what does that make me?"

"An asshole big like this bar," she said. "Now go home to your son, Bruce Konick."

"You know, Minh, I think I know you from somewhere."

She waved two fingers at him as if a magician seeking to make a parakeet disappear.

"I really think I do," he said.

"You know me from drinking in this bar, Bruce Konick. That is all. I only serve you two beers because Skinny feels sorry about your face."

The men in their Carhartts laughed into their beer glasses. He wanted to knock her down and he knew he looked like he did. His eyes went cold, he made them slits. Her lips were painted and she bent a smile, daring him to lay her back over the cheap liquor in the well. He even grabbed around for something to knock her in the head with. *Filthy gook bitch.* Across the bar, the two correctional officers lit cigarettes and grinned wildly at him, smiling until their eyes closed. The fat one with a crew cut and red face shook his match cold.

"You thinking about doing something?" he said

"I know right where I know you from, Minh," Bruce said.

"Set there and finish your beer," said the man.

Malinda waved him quiet.

"Yes, Minh," Bruce said. "I know now. I shot your twin sister in the wire at Khe Sanh and watched the sun turn her black as a nigger."

He smoked and grinned and waited for the men to fall upon him, but there was a long second before they did.

The funeral procession came up Court Street through two red lights while the wind blew rain from the hickories on the courthouse lawn. The old man stopped his pickup truck in traffic, the bed weighed down by a load of birch logs. He stood behind the open door with his cap in his hands and first saw the hearse and the flag-draped casket pass darkly in the windows of the State Savings building. He bowed his head and crossed himself. One by one the dark Fords and Buicks full of old men in their lone suits and gray-haired ladies with fake pearls turned down Grant Street for the drive out to Saint Joseph's Cemetery along the flooding banks of the Watega River. Traffic was now backed up for a block behind him and the drivers lay on their horns, but he would not move until the small procession drove off from sight.

The drivers veered around a birch log fell in the street and cussed him with their fingers. Fat women with back-seats full of fat children called him an old fuck. A teenaged boy wearing a T-shirt in this raw cold told him to shag his bony ass. The old man smiled and waved back like a politician on parade when a Cadillac Seville stopped and reflected him and the courthouse hickories in the door. The passenger window came down electronically. Behind the wheel was a man in a suit looking out at him. His hair was hard from spraynet.

"I'm going after that log right now," the old man said.

"You can't just park in the street while you do it."

The old man laughed at the way the rain beaded on his hairsprayed head.

"You got to move your truck and then get the log," he told him.

"Where I come from we stop for the passing of the dead, and I was born here in 1916. Right out in Saint Marie Township. I remember when Court Street was nothing but bricks."

"There's too much traffic now days, sir."

"The dead are bigger than all the traffic. You'll know what I mean someday."

The man glanced at his watch and cursed under his breath. The cord from a phone was plugged into his cigarette lighter.

"You going to get that log moved before someone blows a tire on it?" he said. "Or am I going to have to flag down a cop?"

"Flag, my ass," the old man said. "You could call one right up on that phone of yours and tell him my name's Bruno Konick and I think that you are one rude son of a bitch."

"What did you call me?"

Bruno Konick stepped closer to the window.

"A rude son of a bitch," he said.

"I'm with the state attorney's office. I could have a cop down here real fast to impound that truck."

"Then maybe you could use that fancy shit phone of yours for something besides ordering a pizza."

The man went red and started to speak, but raised the window with a button and drove away. Bruno laughed to himself and walked out into the street, picking up the log where it lay small and wet along the lane line, the white bark streaked black from the puddle mud. The cars swerved and honked and he waved them all away with his hand. He looked at the log and he looked at the potholes where the standing water mirrored the sky.

"Now them potholes would mess up a tire, you dumb son of a bitch. But not this log."

Bruno took Court Street past the bridge where hockers of bubble gum covered the railing and beneath the Watega River spooled along brown with mud, foam streaked, floating odd driftwood shapes. He drove along Station Street toward the old train depot they were renovating into a restaurant. A long-haired tuckpointer knelt on plastic knee pads and worked mortar into the spaces between the red bricks with a trowel. By the street stood a portable marquee on tires and Bruno parked to read it: *Dance in 1985 at the Stationhouse Bar and Grill.*

He shook his head while a dump truck passed down the block of whiteboard bungalows and vacant storefronts, then studied the limestone platform and the bed of gravel where the rails once set. The tuckpointer hummed over a radio song, cement in his hair. *Who the Christ would want to dance here with all them ghosts?* He found a cigar butt on the floormats and chewed it, remembering the autumn of 1945 when he was among the first men back from the war in Europe to touch this platform with two boots, the same way his father had the winter of 1919 with his lungs scorched from mustard gas and influenza killing half the county, himself happy the A-bombs kept him out of another fight. He saw his sons off to Vietnam here, exactly one year apart, and saw one return scarfaced and the other with trackmarks between his toes and the hypodermic needle hid away in his barracks bag. More than five hundred men probably left from this worn limestone to cross oceans and return dragging wooden legs and lighting Camels with hooked hands. There were boys drowned in rivers and disappeared in jungles and starved in POW camps and vaporized over Tokyo in the glass noses of B-17s. Most returned back-flat in military caskets with a detail of potbellied legionnaires loading them into the beds of Ford pickup trucks, and they were the boys the army and Marine Corps could find. Sometimes there was only a leg in a boot, a head in a helmet. The dead had to die all over again whenever the living came home.

The tuckpointer sang like a howling dog when Bruno rolled down the window.

"They really going to have dancing here?" the old man asked.

"You say something?" the tuckpointer said.

He flipped unused mortar off the trowel and turned back to lower the volume. He looked at Bruno and grinned at this old man and his overloaded truck, then scratched his beard with gloved fingers.

"Are they going to have dancing here?" Bruno said.

"Right on the old platform after we get it walled in. The owners already booked that guy who sounds like George Jones for New Year's Eve."

"You'd have to be a damned ghoul to dance on this platform."

"Why's that?"

"You just would after knowing what I know."

"What the hell are you talking about?"

"Nothing at all," Bruno said. "Don't pay no attention to me."

The tuckpointer rolled his eyes and spat in the gravel before returning to his trowel.

"You interested in buying some cordwood?" Bruno asked.

"Can't use it."

"I'll split it and deliver it right to your house and stack the logs up tight. Just tell me what you want to pay."

The tuckpointer watched himself work.

"I ain't got no fireplace," he said.

"It wouldn't cost as much as you think to build. I could mason you one out of river rocks with a nice hickory mantle so your wife can set pictures on it."

"I ain't got a wife no more."

The tuckpointer turned up the radio. He took a hammer and chisel from his tool belt and began knocking away old mortar.

"You know anybody that might need some wood?" Bruno said.

He pointed to the radio with a hammer.

"I can't hear you," he said. "I can't hear you at all."

It was darkening to the north when Bruno headed for home through the fields of green cornstalks folded upon the furrows from the rain. The Watega River coursed off into the grainy haze, a foul brown length flooded back into the bankside trees. Ahead, the grain elevators of Saint Marie blended with the gray sky and he drove for them until he came to his lane. He looked through the windshield and saw nothing but the rain in the wind and the green leaves falling from the oaks and the elms long before they'd turned their colors. Sticks and birdnests and dead sparrows floated in the ditch water. The ducks would not migrate south this autumn; they were already leaving the river in pairs.

He drove up the puddled ruts toward his tiny clapboard house where stacked about the back lot was the cordwood from a hundred trees. The dogs were barking in their pen, throwing themselves against the chain-link. He saw yellow flames shooting from the rock chimney atop the toolshed, the tar paper roof steaming as if ablaze. Firelight glowed from the open door. He jumped from his truck and the wind took his hat. He grabbed a feed bucket filled with rainwater and ran in the smoky toolshed where his son Bruce lay on the dirt floor, the hearth fire skittering his shadow across the pine wall. Bruno doused the fire and the hiss from the steam was louder than the barking dogs. The shed walls were hung with dated tools restored to the way they had once been. There were scythes and husker's hooks and three pairs of blacksmith's tongs, even a blackened forge in the corner. He dropped the bucket and checked the plow harnesses, glossy with saddle soap. The pieces of the Whizzer engine were strewn upon the tool bench, the rusted carburetor, the small pistons gummed black, the spark plug so old the ceramic casing was cracked in two. He inspected each piece, then kicked Bruce's boot where he lay sleeping heavily on a plaid horse blanket.

"Get up, you son of a bitch."

Bruce raised his cheek and cocked a blackened eye. Blood was dried upon his chin. The steam was dissipating. Bruno yanked away the horse blanket, then dropped it on his son when he felt the vomit. He turned to watch the rain fall upon the wrecked fields.

"I find out you broke into my shed and stole my tools for beer money, I'll call the sheriff my goddamned self. You ain't nothing to me no more. But that boy of yours would rob a church to get the bail money."

His son's scars were caked with mud and vomit.

"Yessir," Bruno said. "Luke would forgive you murder because of them scars. He thinks Vietnam did a number on you—like you are this good father down deep but the war messed you up so he's got to understand."

Bruce came to his knees and sat back against a wagon wheel. He put his face in his hands. The smell of him forced Bruno halfway out the door.

"You don't deserve that boy of yours," Bruno said.

"Luke ain't got the balls he was born with," Bruce said. "He lay there listening to Katie banging Larry Stewart when I was on nights. He heard it for a year and didn't say shit."

"I'm glad Katie is happy."

"You motherfucker."

"Luke thinks you're a hero and all your heroics messed you up in the head. But I knew what you were a long time before Vietnam."

"Then what am I?"

Outside, the rain made the trees appear to be melting.

"I asked you what I am," Bruce said.

"Real lucky that Vietnam come along. Without it, you'd have no excuse for being a fuck-up."

Bruce put his face between his knees and cried.

"Now get off my property before I call the sheriff."

Bruno took a ten dollar bill and dropped it by his son's boot. Then he walked for the house and needed two hands to open the door against the small squall. The house smelled of field mud and cold rain. There was a month's worth of unread newspapers stacked upon a worn sofa, a table beside the window where sat a half-eaten bowl of oatmeal and a fifth of Early Times with an unbroken tax stamp. He knelt by the fireplace masoned from odd river rocks and stuffed kindling between three ash logs and blew cold and soon thin flames spindled around the wood.

He stood by the window when his son came from the toolshed. Bruce went headlong into the wet wind with arms flailing like an unstrung marionette, only mobile, made of flesh, more afflicted. The rain slanted into his scars while he staggered off down the lane, disappearing into the sheets of water. In the fireplace the dry wood cracked and drooled smoke up the flue. Bruno watched the puddles boil for a long time after his son was gone and wondered vaguely why some lives always lead to this end. The dogs lowered their heads in the small house bedded with hay and peered out at the storm with wide, glowing eyes.

Late that night Bruno woke beside the fireplace in his wool covers and only a few orange coals glowed. He lay flat, lost, and very still, the cold in his skin like a fever. His dead wife came to him in a dream and the dream had been so real he believed her with him beneath the blankets, her eyes soft and tranquil as they never were in life, this small woman who hid in her hair and he called *cat* though Catherine was not her name. He closed his eyes and wished her smile was upon his stomach, her black hair spread about his thighs like water running slowly over sand, himself lost in the pale beauty of her breasts. He feared her coming in his dreams only to lie down beside him and die once again. *Like you never wanted it to take you, that cancer you thought was a bird to come fly you away. Your face so drawn and gray, but happy to be leaving for the man dead in the high grass of Guadalcanal where the cloud shadows dapple the blood from his wounds. His name was Tom or Tim and you always made me him whenever I lay with you, your eyes closed and swimming beneath their lids. You left off like heaven was a new town and Len just an infant screaming his face red and Bruce could only point at birds and mumble half words. Goddamn you, woman, I told you that first time to keep your legs from around my waist.*

He coughed from his chest and made sounds not unlike crying. Soon she was gone like the rain upon the roof eaves and there was only the sound of wind punching the window glass. He wiped his eyes and wished the cold dark away when he first saw her, that second snow of peace when *he walked into the streetlight and out again, off toward the Washington Avenue bridge where the snowflakes vanished into the eddy water of the Watega River. He could be away from the town, the pinned coat sleeves of the amputees, the diner counters with young men staring silently into pie cases. He'd walked off to hate them and their stories about fucking bohunk girls for a lone cigarette in the DP camps where filthy, dead-eyed people slept in dog piles against the spring cold. Piss on them, he thought. My life will be more than memories.*

That day he drank at Carlo's Tavern with young men who wore Silver Star pins on their mackinaw collars. They raised beer steins and ate pickled eggs from three-gallon jars. They lit cigarettes, sang dirty barracks songs, these men with soft skin and hard stares getting wall-eyed drunk in the town they fought to see again. Bruno drank with Jimmy Brammer, a boy from Saint Marie who lost an ear on Okinawa and did not have whiskers enough to shave. Jimmy leaned on his elbow and looked at Bruno, telling him about the young war widow from

Charbonneau who liked it from behind, wanted his penis between her breasts, in her mouth, anywhere he had the idea to put it. He got her at the stove, coming out of the bath, sometimes grabbing her hair like a mare's mane and yanking until she smiled and came down to her knees.

"Her husband got it on a troop ship somewhere in the North Atlantic," Jimmy said, a red hole where his ear once was. "A real lucky bastard to get it on the way over. But she's dirty, and I'd guess there's thousands like her all over the country, dirty and crazy as chickens. It puts a guy in the mind to take a real long drive so he can love them all."

Bruno nodded and sipped his beer. Outside, county workmen stood on ladders leaned against the lampposts along Court Street and replaced the wind-tattered flags with the face of Santa Claus. Jimmy talked about the war widow through four rounds of beer, never once saying her name, but ceaselessly describing every interlude. Then he wanted to know what the concentration camps were really like and if the women still had nice breasts because in the newsreels he couldn't tell.

"Some of them had real pretty eyes," he said, "starved as they were. Just like Lauren Bacall."

Bruno smoked and watched himself in the barback mirror. Without warning, he grabbed Jimmy Brammer's hand and winked at him before burning its smooth back with a cigarette.

"Now smell your hand," he said. "Take one big smell and that's what them camps were like."

Jimmy rubbed the blister with a beer mug and called him a crazy son of a bitch. The men along the bar went quiet. Bruno stood and put on his hat and walked out into the snow.

He saw the moon in the dark and in the dark the moon was as bright as this first snow of peace, and as cold. The moments of wind, the moments of calm, and himself trembling from all things except the cold in this river town. How absurd the peace after the war, he thought, with Christmas, with a town expecting us to become farmers again. Will we work fields and nail boards and fire foundry boilers and drift fast to sleep, like building their town and harvesting their food are the spoils? He

26

looked down at the water, as if he could see it in the moments before freezing, when he heard her small feet sliding through the snow. She leaned beside him against the railing. Her long black hair slipped its pins to blow about her shoulders. Moonlight gleamed in her teary eyes. She'd appeared the way a cat will, cautious though unafraid, casing the silence. He wiped the snow from his eyes until he saw her perfectly, this woman closer to forty than thirty, a beauty that took time to find focus. Even in darkness her eyes shone gray like the ice that will slow this river by dawn. He watched the trees tilt from the wind as if when he turned back she might be gone, but she remained, standing upon tiny cat feet, this woman who would become his wife.

When Luke came down the alley behind Skinny's Tap, there was a thin man with a dead eye vomiting over a garbage can. The knees of his jeans were gray from the wet gravel like the weeds that snarled up the cinderblock wall. His bad eye jumped with every heave. Luke waited shyly behind a telephone pole while the man stooped trembling and cleaned his mouth with a palmful of puddle water. He tried looking away at the rain dripping in long drops off the tavern roof, but the man saw him first.

"You know watching a man puke is like watching him shit," the man said.

"No sir," Luke said.

"I ain't asking you no question."

He spoke the words slowly from his wet mouth, sounding like a man with a cheekful of mud. His belt and pants were undone enough for pubic hair to show.

"I'm looking for my dad," Luke said. "Bruce Konick. I ain't seen him in three days and I know he drinks in here."

"What do I look like to you?"

"He's hard to miss," Luke said. "He's got these scars."

"Looks like his face caught on fire and someone tried putting it out with a hatchet."

Luke nodded and flipped up the collar of his field jacket.

"You could say that," he said.

"I can say anything I want to," the man said.

"Thank you."

"I can open my mouth and say suck a nigger trucker's dick. I could yell it if I fucking wanted."

The man lay down facing the wall upon the gray weeds and began coughing. The rain from the eaves dripped on his head.

Luke walked off down the alley, looking for his father's red Pontiac where it might be parked behind the taverns. A slattern fog settled over the wood-frame rooftops and veiled the cars passing down Station Street so they were only vague headlights coming ahead of engine noise. He searched for his father behind dumpsters and in backyards where rainwater stood halfway up swing-set slides. He walked to the chain-link fence around Roper Stove and watched the workmen board windows with new plywood while the forklift drivers moved the huge stamping machines up the metal ramps of flatbed trailers. He lit a cigarette, then turned from the fence, looking into the car windows after they came through the fog even if they weren't red Pontiacs.

He went by the courthouse lawn where the Union Soldier stood guard over the fallen hickory branches. The bronze was long turned green but marred with fresh graffiti from the Class of 1984. The streets ran black with water. He came to the Marine Corps recruiting office and behind the storefront window was a cardboard marine with a saber lifted in full salute. Luke stared into his blue eyes, making himself

29

rigid, then practiced a salute with an imaginary sword on the empty sidewalk. He was doing it a third time, imagining the metal coming between his eyes, only an inch from his face, when the recruiting sergeant came out of the door in his khaki shirtsleeves. The wind blew the bottom of his clamped tie. He eyed Luke from a pock-marked face, then nodded.

"You want to come inside, son?" he asked. "I got free coffee. It's even drinkable for not being made by a mess sergeant."

Luke felt uneasy when he looked at the sergeant because he knew what the ribbons meant he wore rowed above his left pocket. The navy cross. The purple heart with two oak-leaf clusters. The Vietnam service ribbon. The gold parachutists wings of Marine Corps Force Reconnaissance. Luke kept his hands in his pockets and stared timidly at his boots.

"You got to buy them swords?" he said.

"That's Lance Corporal Turner, our marine of the year," the sergeant said. "You ever see President Reagan getting off his helicopter, you'll see Turner giving him a salute."

"I was just wondering about his sword."

"The corps gives them as awards. I got mine for being a squad leader at Hue. That was in Vietnam."

"I know all about Hue," Luke said. "That was during the Tet Offensive in 1968. I read all the books I could find about it at the high school. My dad was at Khe Sanh about the same time you was at Hue."

"That his field jacket?"

"Yessir. He was a corporal when he got wounded. A gook sapper got him with a grenade and scarred his face real bad. He don't got but a hole for an ear. You get your navy cross fighting around the citadel there at Hue?"

The sergeant nodded, then crossed his arms and put each hand under an armpit. He blew cold.

"You know why Turner has red stripes down his pant legs?" the sergeant said.

"It's for the blood shed at Tampico during the Mexican War. The marines come ashore in these wooden boats and stormed the place. You got to be a lance corporal or higher to wear them stripes."

"You sure you don't want to come inside?"

"They give them dress blues to you?" Luke asked.

"No. They're special. You have to have them tailored."

"What do they give you?"

"You got it all wrong, son. The question is what you will give the Marine Corps."

"If I joined up," Luke said, "could I stay with my buddy?"

The sergeant smiled without showing teeth.

"We win wars that way," he said.

"I got to go to work now, but I'll come back."

"You bring your buddy with you."

"Yessir," Luke said.

He walked for the warehouses of Bade Appliance down East Avenue while dump trucks loaded with gravel trundled over the potholed street. He hoped there would be semi-trailers to unload, shipments of boxed refrigerators and stoves, maybe an easy day of dining-room sets and VCRs. The morning was nearly dark and the yellow streetlight glowed upon his jacket sleeves. Outside the window of Bray's Diner he looked past the tables at the long coffee bar where his mother hurried with steaming plates of eggs, moving between the orange heat lamps and the booths full of laborers who eyed her breasts coming and her backside going away. The Mexican cooks hit the order bells and the old men at the bar waved their cigarettes like wands. Her chestnut hair was wound into a bun. Her face was tired and drawn in the stark diner light. *I hope this ain't the happiness you left for.*

Men and boys were gathered behind the warehouse where a fire made from pallet slats burned inside the incinerator. They drank soda from cans and dressed in a motley of denim and military surplus. A few sat smoking on upturned loading carts and nodded to Luke as he came up the alley. He went off between the warehouses, the walls scrawled with spray-painted graffiti. A black man leaned against the wall beside the loading dock, studying a clipboard. His Carhartt jacket would not zip over his stomach.

"The money easy today, Cecil?" Luke asked.

"No, tomcat," he said. "The whore's easy, but the money's always hard."

Cecil glanced up at the small rain leaning through the fog and shook his head.

"Nothing like working in a piss storm," he said. "Four days now."

Luke put his hands in his pockets and grinned.

"How many trucks you got coming this morning?" he asked.

"Not enough to keep all these motherfuckers busy until three."

"Shit," Luke said.

"You got to be here early, tomcat. You know how the man works it."

"You can't write me in?"

"I wouldn't want to see one of these old boys whip your bony ass."

Cecil pulled a Kool from his Carhartt pocket. His fingernails were long but clean.

"Your old man turn up?" he said.

"Not in four days," Luke said.

Cecil looked at Luke and blew smoke through his nose.

"I walked the A Shau Valley until my feet was hamburger and my eyes no bigger than mouse turds. I got me two purple hearts in the drawer where I keep my underwear. But I ain't no wildman running all over town talking about the gooks who shot me up."

"I don't know," Luke said.

"Listen, tomcat. Vietnam didn't make one motherfucker crazy who wasn't crazy before he got there. You know what I'm telling you?"

Luke nodded.

"You need some money?" Cecil said.

"I got enough."

"Then get in early tomorrow. The money's easy all day. We got us seven trucks coming in with kitchen tables."

Luke waved goodbye and went east past the old brick-yard. He climbed the muddy berm where the railroad tracks coursed toward the wide sky and the cornstalks lay beaten down by the rains. Few birds flew between their nests in the telephone poles. At Leggtown Road he walked slowly east with his thumb in the air. In the fields the rain-water pooled about the drowned corn and he thought the clouds were jagged mountains though he knew this not to be true.

The last time Luke saw his father was the morning the rains first came. The thunderheads moved down the Watega River from the north and the downpour flattened the sowed fields of the county. Within an hour, the summer became late autumn. He sat at the kitchen table in the sad bungalow his mother left while lightning flares left traces against the morning dark. He smoked the last cigarette slowly when his father fell through the door like a tree cut by axes, cussing the Vietnamese that tossed the grenade into his hole at Khe Sanh. The rain beaded on his gnarled cheek and made rivulets of his scars. He staggered to his feet and fell backward, looking at Luke long enough to slow his reeling eyes, then ran for the toilet with beer vomit spilling between his fingers. Luke covered his ears while his father puked in shifts and called God a gook-loving motherfucker because he knew the silence would come before he broke the mirror holding his reflection. By that night he was gone again, his hand cut from the glass.

Soon the sky tore open and the rain fell with violence. When a pickup truck slowed beside him he'd not heard it. An old farmer with a white mustache yellowed by nicotine rolled down the window. He peered out into the rain and two cur dog faces looked on from behind him.

"You broke down?" he said.

"No, sir. I'm just walking out to Saint Marie."

The farmer looked at the seething ditch water, then at Luke.

"That's eight goddamned miles," he said.

"I know."

"You always been crazy?"

"I guess."

"Guess, shit. There's lightning flying around like nip fighter pilots and if a bolt hits you, you'll die in this ditch with your fillings welding your mouth closed."

The dogs cocked back their ears and one had the face of a raccoon and he barked.

"Sir," Luke said, "my grandpa lives in Saint Marie. Bruno Konick. You know him?"

"Since the third grade," he said. "Get under the tarp in the bed. You can ride on them sacks of dog food."

"Thank you, sir."

"Why the hell you still standing there grinning? You can thank me when the sun's out."

"Yessir."

"Then quit sirring me and get the hell in," he said.

Luke put his foot on the bumper, then swung his other leg over the gate. The old man was driving while he crawled under the canvas tarp with rubber ducking to sit on twenty-pound gunny sacks of dry dog food. The exhaust from the tailpipe rose and twisted in the rain like woodsmoke. The old man cursed the dogs for growling

He held the tarp closed about his cheeks and looked out at the ruined country. The corn was slaughtered. He remembered the summer nights with his mother when they watched the moon wash the fields white from the back porch. The wind rushed in the young corn leaves like the coming of surf. The crickets fell mute and the country became very still after the winds. She asked him if he heard the corn growing. He listened until the nightbirds called from the locust trees, making himself believe he heard the unfolding of leaf and stalk. But even then she was not truly with him. She found love with another man and in his dreams Luke saw him

34

touching her and he knew by her distant smile that this man and his hands made her feel very beautiful.

The last summer night Luke spent with her was almost three years gone. They stood barefoot in the grass and stared at the sky where the dead stars burned for one thousand years. He wondered which stars they were and guessed he'd never know, when she turned to him, the wind twisting her brown hair. *Vietnam only did it to his face and I told him a long time ago that my love had nothing to do with what I see. But it is not love he wants. It is revenge. I thought he wanted to find the Vietnamese and kill him and get his face back like it was. But he wanted revenge a long time before Vietnam.* Luke looked for her eyes but she was gone into her hair as if behind a waterfall. *I can't quit him, he said. I ain't going nowhere with you.* He finally found her eyes but she did not see him. She seemed only her outside. An empty cocoon on a hidden scrub twig. The cracked shell of a locust clasped to hickory bark. His mother smiled in the dark as if this man was there touching her breasts. She was beautiful and he did not wish to break her silence. *Had she ever been my mother at all?*

The farmer turned down Route One where a skein of oak leaves covered the ditch water. The dogs splattered drool on the back window. Their snouts were in the air so that Luke knew the farmer was singing and they were howling. The truck stopped at his grandfather's lane and Luke climbed down from the bed. The farmer leaned out his window, his face red in the dark morning. He took off his hat so the wind would not get it.

"You tell Bruno that Jack Hatcher says he's a pecker as long as the Illinois winter," he said.

"Why's that, sir?"

The farmer grinned so that his eyes half closed.

"After sixty years," he said, "I couldn't get all the reasons in my truck."

He looked like he might say something else, but he didn't, and only waved and drove south toward Chebanse. Luke raised a hand.

The dogs came barking from the wood pile and their forelegs were stained with mud. After seeing it was Luke, they ran back for the toolshed and barked for the old man. Woodsmoke spooled from the rock chimney. Luke walked past the dogs and dropped a hand to pet each one. In the shed, his grandfather worked sandpaper against a rusted bicycle frame clamped upright in two vises bolted into the workbench. The old man stood with his face close to the crossbar where he sanded, looking hard at it after his paper passed. He checked the vise levers for tightness, then the rags protecting the frame from the teeth. Luke pulled the door closed and his jacket steamed from the fire. The old man did not look up until he was done. His eyes were very green and quiet, half lost in the deep seams of his face.

"If you ain't a tomcat," he said.

"I could whip your ass for getting Cecil started on that," Luke said. "He won't give it up."

"It's what you are. You stay gone for days and then here you are—all wet and hungry with your head hanging low."

His grandfather laughed and shook his head, then undid the tie string of his denim apron. He wore three flannel shirts and a letterman's sweater from the high school.

"Grandpa," Luke said, "when you going to buy a coat?"

"A coat's just like this, only it's all sewed together."

"Shit."

"Let me get myself up wind. Was that Jack Hatcher dropped you off?"

"He picked me up on Leggtown Road," Luke said. "He sang to them dogs the whole way and they were singing back. His face was red like he was whiskey drunk. I'd bet he was."

"His face has been red since the Coral Sea," the old man said. "A Jap kamikaze hit his ship and lit him on fire. But him with those dogs is something to see. His wife couldn't have babies, but not from lack of trying, Jack says. They made every dog and cat on the farm into babies. There's people like that in the world."

"His face didn't look that bad."

"It didn't get him home. But you'd piss yourself to hear Jack tell the story."

The old man smiled and took a fifth of Early Times from the bench where it sat between coffee cans filled with wrenches and screwdrivers. He poured three fingers into a tinware cup. Luke took it and sipped from the metal rim.

"You see him?" he said. "He ain't been home since these storms started."

"Tonight we're supposed to have another. Then the cold and snow are coming."

Luke watched the old man check the engine parts soaking in a mop bucket full of solvent. By themselves, they looked useless. He fished out a small carburetor and cleaned it with a wire brush. The solvent cut through the grease on his large hands and made them very white.

"I take it you saw him," Luke said.

The old man worked the brush hard.

"This here is the carburetor off a Whizzer motor bike," he said. "That's the frame in the vises. Back in 1930, every boy in America wanted one of these. I just got mine a week ago."

Luke cracked the door and lit a cigarette.

"What's a wizard have to do with him?" he asked.

"It's called a Whizzer and this little engine will fit to the frame by a couple springs."

"Why ain't you answering me?"

"I'm going to have to do some horse trading to get those springs."

"You know he's got a Purple Heart?"

"It sure beats the hell out of a white cross. Now go dry your ass and we'll get us a couple of steaks up at Bertrand's."

Luke leaned in the doorway while the firelight twisted his shadow about the jamb. The old man turned back to the tool bench and refolded the sandpaper before resuming work on the frame. He worked slow, but with method. Luke blew smoke out into the rain before he walked toward the house with the dogs biting at his ankles as if he were a sheep to be herded.

* * *

The old man led him up Sherman Street with his hands deeply pocketed against the cold. They turned down Sheridan past the laundromat where dark-eyed Mexican women toted infants and garbage bags of dirty clothes up the wooden steps. The one traffic light in town swung from the wind, and the powerline it dangled from roosted wet pigeons. They went up the cracked sidewalk where dead weeds snarled and headed toward Bertrand's Café. Luke watched the old man look into all the windows of the empty store-fronts as if there was something to see. The café and the coin laundry were the only businesses still open. He held the café door open for the old man and waited for him to notice, then followed him inside and they took a booth in front.

Luke smoked while the old man stared out the window with his veiny hands folded on the table. Art Bertrand came over from behind the empty counter with the coffee pot and they turned over their cups. His teeth were dark yellow from nicotine as was the ceiling of the diner. He poured the coffee and waited.

"What the hell, Bruno?" Art said. "I guess I could forget I got a restaurant to run and stand here all afternoon gawking at your pretty face."

"A woman once told me I look like a Greek god," the old man said.

"Or a goddamned Greek."

The old man smiled and rolled his eyes. He looked around the diner.

"That's your prejudice talking, Art," he said. "Them Greeks sure know how to make a restaurant. I'll give them that."

"I'd stack this place with dynamite before I'd sell it to a Greek," Art said. "This is about the last restaurant in the county they don't own."

"They give you four eggs when you order two," the old man said. "Ain't bad from my end."

"That's some foreign bullshit. In America if a man orders two eggs I figure that's what you should give him."

"That ain't your prejudice, Art. It's your cheapness."

"I think them Greeks are over here buttering us up so they can steal our secrets."

"What, Art? That you need six prunes every morning when you only admit to three?"

Art Bertrand took the coffee pot off the table where he'd set it and looked at Luke.

"You know, Luke, every year Saint Marie has a personality contest and every year your grandpa wins it hands down."

"It's all right, Mister Bertrand," Luke said. "I'll shoot him before he starts wanting that flaming cheese."

"Mister Bertrand," Bruno said. "Shit. Art just get us a couple of steaks with fries before my grandson starts saluting you."

The old man took a hand-rolled cigarette out of his shirt pocket and stared out the window while he struck the match. The tow truck from Emme's hauled a wrecked Ford pickup through the puddles.

"I bet you could get that engine cheap," he said. "Maybe half a hundred."

"Don't tell me you didn't see him," Luke said. "You ain't much of a liar."

The old man stirred his black coffee for a long time.

"I bet the engine don't got but fifty thousand miles on it."

"I'd like to know what he did to you?" Luke said.

"Besides get so drunk he pisses himself on barstools? I think all them boys who went to Vietnam would rather cry than work. I'll just leave it at that."

"Is my Uncle Len like him?"

The old man took the spoon from the cup and laid it steaming on the table.

"You won't even talk about him, will you?" Luke said.

"You take to shooting dope, I won't talk about you either."

"Shit."

"You thought any more about moving in with me and going out to that community college?" the old man said. "I'd get you a car."

"With what?"

39

"I said I'd get you a car."

Luke sat in the booth watching old man talk about everything he was not thinking.

"I saw the Marine Corps recruiter this morning," Luke said.

The old man looked at him, then looked out the window again.

"I'd just as soon put you out of misery here and now," he said. "I'd hate to see you turn into one of those sadistic assholes."

"Someone's got to defend this country."

The old man laughed out loud.

"No, Grandpa," Luke said. "The Russians. Cuba. What if the Mexicans went communist and joined up with them? I saw this movie where they dropped all these paratroopers in Colorado and then come up through Texas in tanks."

"They wouldn't make it ten miles into Texas," the old man said. "Down there even the women can shoot straight."

"I'm being serious."

"My ass."

"It could happen," Luke said.

"Then what's stopping you from enlisting?"

Luke went silent. He tapped the saltshaker against the table. The old man looked past him and smoked and waited for Art to bring their four-dollar steaks.

Len Konick and the Mexican girl came up the graystone stairs and then down a narrow hallway of broken floorboards. They were off the Chicago streets now, out of the wind and the rain. She took small steps behind him, dressed in a white leather jacket with fringe, quiet the way he found her pacing the puddles beyond the swollen hoops of streetlight. He led her to the small apartment he rented and remembered the wet nights in Saigon when men stood lined outside the cinderblock brothels and drank tin quarts of beer. They were infantrymen with soaked faces, granted twenty-four hours away from the firebases. Some nights the line was very long and the men had ten minutes and it was enforced by MPs with batons. He saw them between his shifts at the hospital where he worked the ward for the newly amputated as an orderly. He walked heroin high those wet nights, through the sea of dark-eyed children reaching into his pockets, the MPs throwing grenades down into the sewers to kill the Viet Cong, imagining what these men looked like to a whore. The warm beer shining from their teeth. Their sweaty faces glowing in the dark heat. Len knew he looked different to this Mexican girl, so very different.

Her mouth was wet when she came into the apartment with two windows and a bed that pulled down from the wall. There were heaps of jeans and workshirts stained with brick dust on the floor. In the sink were a bowl and spoon, a saucepan soaking off pork and beans.

Len touched her cheek but she turned away. Her black hair fell over her eyes. He took the folded bills from his shirt pocket, fifty-eight dollars. She grabbed the money from his hand without watching herself, then put the bills into her jeans pocket.

"Is that enough for an hour?" Len asked.

"You can do anything but kiss me," she said.

"Will you undress in the window?"

She walked to the bed and took off her sweatshirt as if a clown preparing for a show. Her back was pale in the smears of streetlight. When she faced him, she brushed her hair away from her breasts and circled her palm about her stomach and there amid the rain sounds the girl became a prostitute. He quickly undressed. She closed her eyes and stroked the undersides of her breasts. He stayed her hand when she went to undo her jeans, then laid her down beside him and covered them with a wool blanket. He brought her arm around him and held her cold body.

"The moon was like the noonday sun in the window when my brother Bruce raped me. He came down the hallway dragging his feet. I lay small and still upon my bed. At fourteen Bruce already drank bourbon in the way of men. He loved knives. He ran traps along the creek banks for muskrat and raccoon even though he had no way of selling the pelts. He once made a spear from a hickory stick and a jagged flintstone and walked off into the dusk and returned by dawn with a yearling doe over his shoulders. Our mother died of cancer when I was an infant. Our father worked nights at Gould Foundry firing the boilers. He was left to be wild. I lived as a victim of his moods.

"That night I heard him and another boy laughing drunk when they sat on his bed. They smelled of sweat and whiskey and river mud. I pretended I was asleep. The wind sounded like rain in the leaves of the cherry tree and the curtains billowed and the gusts scattered the birds to circle about the fields. I opened an eye. They were masturbating, their hands and organs exaggerated upon the moonlit wall. They rose with full erections, these two boys with the hard bodies of men. I was pinned upon my stomach while nausea overtook me, the sets of hands hard on my back. I closed my eyes until I saw spots. Like a starry night, I thought. So much like a starry night.

"We never spoke about that night. It could have happened to other people. I bled from my rectum and when that bleeding stopped, the bleeding I only felt started. My father is the kind of man who has known too much sadness to understand that other people also suffer. Telling him would have pushed him deeper inside himself. Maybe he would have killed Bruce. He is a stoic man but not unjust."

The girl lay on the mattress with her hand cold against his arm. She looked as if she'd fallen there. He closed his eyes and then opened them, feeling her slow breath on his cheek.

"In Vietnam I gave morphine shots to men in sweaty blue pajamas who lay staring off in hospital beds. They missed legs, an arm, maybe only a foot. There were men who thought they still had hands to swat the flies off their lips. Some wiggled their stumps and bit like horses at the insects while others paid the flies no mind and gazed at the floor fans spinning hard at the ends of the ward. I kept them all very high.

"My brother was at Khe Sanh with the Marine Corps. We never wrote. I only knew of his life by the few letters our father sent. There was a boy among the amputees who resembled Bruce though they looked nothing alike. This boy was blond, my brother was dark. I knew they understood the world as a place where you can take if no man uses violence to say you cannot have. For them, God is true force, and I am not sure they are wrong.

"This boy lost his legs from a land mine while sweeping the Iron Triangle with the First Infantry Division. He kept a shoebox full of pictures beneath his bed. There were fifty stills of dead Vietnamese with their penises cut off and shoved in their mouths like cigars. The dead were mostly old men and boys, a few NVA regulars in khaki uniforms, even a woman without breasts. He shuffled through the pictures and called them dead cocksuckers. He held them up one after the other for the men on the ward until nobody wanted to see them anymore. The men shunned him, requested curtains, joked openly about running him AWOL. He tried to interest the nurses. He then looked at the pictures alone, lost in a morphine haze, and looked at his bandaged stumps.

"It was in this time that my brother was wounded at Khe Sanh. My father wrote me, five lines in pencil. I believed that God had marked him like Cain and I myself believed in God so profoundly that I spoke with him long into the night. My prayers were answered. But acts of justice are like acts of brutality—they are truly random. Life has taught me that if God is at all, He only watches. I did not know this for many years after I read my father's letter, so for a time I was very happy. All men would know of Bruce's sin and turn away and leave him to his darkness.

"My euphoria did not last. Three days after I received the letter, the blond boy killed himself in the night. When the nurse found him dead in the morning dark, Avery and I wheeled over a curtain to block him off from the rest of the ward. Cravis Avery was the other orderly on my shift, a gentle black from the South who swore that after his discharge from the army he would buy land in the woods, never talk to

44

a soul, and live off the rabbits he shot in the brush piles. His dark face dripped sweat while he pulled the sheet off the blond boy. The hypodermic needle was slanted into his arm. The shoebox full of pictures was gone from under his bed. Avery pulled the needle from his vein and dropped it into a metal bowl. We moved the blond boy from the bed to the gurney. The body sagged at the waist and the stumps were very cold.

"'You got him the morphine,' I said.

"Avery nodded and closed the eyes with his finger and thumb.

"'The womens ain't got no love for a gimp,' he said. 'Even if he has a gallon of sweet wine and ten reefers.'

"I covered the body with a sheet. Sweat ran down Avery's cheeks like tears.

"'He was sick bastard,' I said.

"'What's a kid like this going to do when he gets home?'

"I was silent.

"'No man can go through life without pussy because pussy is life,' Avery said."

Len stopped talking and looked past the girl at the rooftops in the rain. Dark sky, dark city.

"Has a man ever told you these things?" he asked.

The girl lifted her arm to the window, looking at her watch in the vague light. The rain shadows streaked her skin.

"Is there something you want me to do?" she said. "You have ten minutes."

"Will you come tomorrow night?"

"Yes," she said.

Len listened for a trace of something in her voice but there was nothing. She climbed over him and dressed with her back to his face, then checked her pocket for the bills before she left through the door. The streetlight turned bright outside the window and the contour of the light in glass shone on the opposite wall. He rose and followed her to the door, locked it, then lay back down and touched himself softly as if he were his own lover.

45

In the night his brother came to him while he slept. His face was without scars and he walked toward him through a muddy field and smiled as he never had in life. In the dream he knew that his brother was already dead. His body lay in the snow and his face was scarred. Deer fed on frozen corn about his head as if it were a fallen tree. The world of the dream was of two seasons at once. Bruce was dead in the cold dark of Watega County, though he stood transfigured in air daylit and white with wind coming gentle through the trees. Len tried to wake many times because he knew this was a dream, but the dream itself held him to sleep. When Len finally spoke to Bruce, his brother only laughed, as if saying that in death the marks that men believe God gave them for their sins mean nothing. Bruce turned and walked for the budding river trees. Len yelled out, wondering why his brother did not seek forgiveness. Bruce smiled and said that by dying we are made equal because in death, what man needed the idea of God?

The morning came cold and found Len Konick stacking old bricks for salvage upon wooden pallets. The wrecking ball had turned the old foundry to rubble after a fire burned there for three days. The piles of burst concrete were charred black. The metal forming rods lay twisted about the lot like deformed skeletons. He watched a black man, an ex-convict they called Jabo, take up a brick and knock off the mortar with a hammer. An old black sat on a pallet already stacked, inert like a bird roosting on a power line. He wore layers of coats and a filthy fedora and warmed the taped bottoms of wingtips against a smoldering burn barrel. Len knew him only as Preacher. Jabo stacked three more bricks and wiped off his wet face with a coat sleeve, his left eye swollen shut. He was shod in prison boots though he'd been paroled a year. He smiled at Len, his nostrils big around as thumbs.

"I've been stacking bricks with Preacher for six months," he said. "The old nigger always work the same damned way. He gets out here first thing and does his one pallet. Then he sits his ass down and waits for the man to give him his eight dollars. Ain't that right, Preacher?"

The old man said nothing. He stared off through the woodsmoke twisting from the barrel. Len shook his head and made rows of wet bricks by stacking them two long, two across. Jabo tied off his hood and spat.

"Preacher sure hopes the man comes before noon," he said. "Then he gets off early to the projects with a gallon of wine under each arm."

"I give the sacrament to the sick," Preacher said.

"The holy motherfucking bone is what you give," Jabo said.

"I don't give no wine that ain't been blessed by Him."

"Shit. You buy any wine them Arabs on Cottage Grove is making a deal like Monte Hall."

Jabo drank the bottom from a half pint of gin and eyed the wrecking ball rising high before being released straight down upon a ruined wall. The bricks were salvaged by crews of stooped blacks, gaunt men dressed in a motley of clothes and hats, warming their legs by open fires. Jabo grinned and took aim with the bottle against a chain-link fence. The force of the throw opened the thin scab below his eye.

"Your eye is bleeding," Len said.

Jabo touched the eye and then looked at his hand.

"The motherfucker got a lucky shot," he said. "I opened the door and there it came."

"You fighting with Charles again?" Len asked.

"That bitch motherfucker. Hell no. My old cellmate jumped me drunk. I was coming into the liquor store and there the nigger was."

Preacher shook his head. He stared down a crow on the fence, undisturbed by the noise from the wrecking ball.

"You got to forgive that man," he said. "Him and her both."

Jabo waved Preacher away with his hand. He looked at Len as if they were two sober men in the company of a drunk.

"I spend three years with this nigger at Stateville," Jabo said, "smelling his farts and listening to him beat his shit in the jailhouse dark. He says he wants a picture of a real woman because no niggers he knows ever banged a white bitch from *Playboy*. The nigger says he can't dream that way no more. He wants a real black woman so he can look into her eyes while he does his thing. I feel bad for him. He don't got nobody sending him shit on the inside. Not even his momma. So I let him use Tamikka's picture and he gets paroled before I do. You know what the nigger does? He goes and finds her and they start kicking it that night."

"So you want her back?" Len said.

"Hell no," Jabo said. "I want to shoot them both in the face. You know, leave my name on their cheeks forever."

"You'd kill them?"

"Not the way I'd do it."

"You ain't free until you forgive them both," Preacher said.

Jabo lit a half-smoked cigarette.

"This old boy can't even read fuck on the shithouse wall," he said. "He don't know a U from a C so I know he ain't read the Bible. But he's got twenty fool niggers thinking he full of the Holy Ghost."

The old man sat like a stone.

The snack truck came up the street through the mist and jumped the curb and parked along the chain-link fence. The driver wore a nylon snowsuit and walked about the truck as if his legs never straightened. He opened hatches to display his wares of pizza slices, burritos, a coffee urn the size of a howitzer shell. The salvagers began milling about the truck to haggle with the driver over the price of a mashed donut. Jabo studied the crowd, his eye wet with blood.

"Shit," he said, "I see one, two, damn," he said. "I see three niggers that owe me fifty cents."

He climbed from the ruined foundation and ran for the truck like a dog overwhelmed by smell. He waved his arms, cussing the blacks who hoped to have their one dollar spent before he noticed the line. He pulled a burnt two-by-four off a heap of jagged concrete on his way.

Len smoked a cigarette while Preacher took from his pocket a mustard sandwich that was wrapped in newsprint. He chewed, humming hymns mutely, his legs nearly wrapped around the burn barrel.

"How'd you come to be a preacher?" Len said.

The old man stopped chewing. The wrecking ball swung violently against the last standing wall. The red bricks burst.

"I saw my brother Davis killed over a shovel," he said.

Preacher paused, but not to let Len speak. He wrapped up his sandwich and put what was left back into his pocket.

"It happened in 1928, back in Hope Mills, North Carolina. We worked dawn until dusk laying down gravel on a railroad gang. There was a white man named John McGee who'd won him some medals for killing in France. Used to say it like that, too. The company painted lines on the handles of the shovels the colored used and McGee was particular about not touching anything after us. I know he picked Davis out because he was a small man and Davis was a big one. He started accusing my brother of touching his shovel in the tool cart. Davis was quiet and McGee took it as him being disrespectful, but Davis never could make a word when he got scared. My brother was a young boy like me and he never did nothing against the law or white men. He stood there trying to talk for himself and started crying. Then McGee killed him with a white man's shovel, stabbed him in the throat with it and laid him dead. The colored men held me down. They picked Davis up and carried him over to the shade and left him against this rock with his head sagged and his throat bloody like a hog cut to bleed."

"What happened to McGee?" Len said.

"He told the sheriff it was self-defense. Lied right to him about how he thought Davis was loony enough to kill. They never did put the law on him. Most of the colored went back to work in the morning. I ran off to Georgia and did the same kind of work for a man named Tom Kennedy. I saw him hit a colored boy so hard his eyeball flew off into the weeds like it was a grasshopper. I never knew what it was about. We was getting fifty cents a day so I kept to my shovel."

"So why are you a preacher?" Len said.

The old man stood from the load of bricks and put his hands against the flames.

"Because without God," he said, "you can't help seeing apes when you look at men."

"So you forgave them?"

"Forgave them and repented for ever hating," Preacher said.

"You can do that?" Len asked.

The old man eyed the backs of his ashen hands as if studying a map.

"You might not think it's what a man should do," Preacher said.

"I wouldn't be able to say," Len said. "Not at all."

He lay with the Mexican girl while squad cars came up Canalport in the rain. The blue lights spun and strafed against the window so that their shadows moved between the four walls. He asked her to hold him and she did, but he felt like the rain being turned by the glass. Her breasts were very cold against his bare back.

"There was this retarded boy who lived across the field from my father named Larry Parton. He went to school with us in Saint Marie. I was ahead of him by a grade but Larry was older than me by a year. His eyes swam so he could never really look at you. Boys were always giving him candy bars to piss on the rectory windows or masturbate a dog. He even ate mud out of the creek for a quarter.

"One time Larry and I were playing catch with my brother. Bruce threw the football so hard that it bounced off the road and rolled into the ditch, down into the mud and cockleburs. He told Larry to go get the ball, that he better move his ass over to the ditch. Larry grinned and laughed through his nose. He even slapped his knees. Bruce walked up to him and asked what the fuck was so funny. I told my brother it was Larry's way. He thought you were joking whenever you told him anything. Bruce looked at him and said, 'You better get that ball before I smack the shit out of you.' Larry laughed like it was the funniest thing he ever heard.

"Bruce could have dropped it right there because he saw that Larry didn't understand what he wanted. But he went and punched him in the face. Blood flew out of Larry Parton's mouth and he knelt down in the field and stood. He put his arm up to his lips and bit his coat sleeve. His eyes shook and welled with tears. He turned and ran across the field for home. Bruce walked over to the ditch after the ball and cursed Larry so loudly that blackbirds sprung cawing from the hedgerow. I never looked at him after that.

"Our father knew what kind of boy Bruce was. Most people did by the way he looked at you with half-closed eyes. All my life, I heard priests and teachers wondering what was wrong with him. But my father is a man who can make himself blind by not looking. He refused to see him truthfully, even after Bruce stole the Luger pistol he brought back from the war and ran away for three days and killed two horses and a milk cow in Andy Janick's barn. You see, my father has spent his adult life trying to forget things of which he never spoke. He knew the war in Europe so intimately that even speaking about it would be like telling the secrets of a lover. But there is more, and I have spent my life trying to figure it out.

"His name is Bruno Konick and he hid from his memories by collecting tools so old that men have forgotten their uses. He owns forges and hammers and clamps he bought from the widows of blacksmiths. He has hammers and chisels once used by limestone masons to score rock for the foundations of farmhouses. He polishes leather plow straps and harnesses though no man will ever again till the land behind a horse. He chops down trees with an ax and tries to sell cordwood to men who warm themselves with gas heat.

He prefers the light from lanterns. He can mason fireplaces from river rock though this trade has never earned him a living. In the winter, he sleeps by the fire the way he did as a boy.

"I asked him once why he collected old tools. He looked at me with his green eyes and smiled. He showed me a hook once used for husking corn. It had the original leather strap and he fastened it to his hand. He demonstrated how the hook was used on a brick. 'A man pulled the husk off this way,' he said. 'The hook was part of his hand for two weeks and for those two weeks it was more valuable than a diamond. He only made enough with it to eat through the winter and plant in the spring. Without it, he ate nothing. Now the grandsons of these men see this hook as junk.'

"I have not seen my father in thirteen years and neither have I seen the scarred face of my brother. For a time, I thought heroin was a gift from God. It ran pain from me the way rivers run white over rocks. We called it the big mother, the busty lover, the big-hipped woman with lips so wet. I smuggled heroin home from Vietnam in four toothpaste tubes as did all the men who learned to use; the army let it all pass. When I came back to Watega County, my brother had left his wife and his young son. Our father never asked me about Vietnam; none of the veterans of his war ever did. They only looked silently at their sons the way they always had—forever mute about themselves and quieter still about the war they sent us to fight. If my father's generation believes anything, it is that all men must take their turn."

When the girl rose, she dressed in stony silence and kept her back to him. The night turned cold after the rain quit. The yellowlit rain upon the windowpanes was shadowed across her shoulders until the wind gusted, drying the glass. He was naked beneath the wool blanket. She left quickly like a cat who had been locked the whole day in a closet. He lay a long time with the door open, hugging himself warm and tight.

The hypodermic needle and the rubber band fell in the sink when his father beat the bathroom door open with a tire iron. His face was wet from vomit. He watched the wood splinter, thinking he was not in a bathroom at all, but among dead corn stalks stitched out of the snow where paired crows circled in the sky, mocking his wandering. He looked for a rock to knock them from the gray light. He looked for sticks. He was listening to the wind sound in their wings when his father looked at the hypo and then at his arm, as if trying to imagine the bulged vein, the needle slantwise in it.

"He raped me," he said. "I bled from my asshole."

His father took up a handful of his shirt and punched him. He tasted bile in his throat. He ducked the crows.

"You have ten minutes to be gone," his father said.

In the morning, Bruno Konick and his grandson loaded the truck with saws and axes and drove out east of the house. It was cold and the sun rose graylit and very round behind the twists of black cloud. He drove for the river woods and handed Luke a sack of Bugler tobacco and rolling papers while he sipped thermos coffee from a canteen cup. There were hints of blue in Luke's brown eyes, this tall stocky boy in layers of flannel shirts and a Marine Corps field jacket. Luke looked at the sack in the palm of his hand, then took a pack of Marlboros from his pocket.

"I got some store-bought ones right here," Luke said.

"Them are the kind with filters."

"I can break the filter off."

"Shit," Bruno said. "I'd of asked you for it if that was what I wanted. Roll me a Bugler."

"I can't read your mind," Luke said. "I ain't no genie in the lamp."

Luke smiled and busted the filter off a Marlboro. Bruno took the cigarette and tried pushing in the tuning knob for the radio like it was the lighter. Luke laughed and drew his cigarette lit off a match.

"For a second there I thought you went dipshit."

"Piss on you, boy," Bruno said. "Someday you'll be able to hide your Easter eggs. I'll be the ghost in the corner laughing my ass off."

"A ghost don't got an ass."

"So it never has to go to the can and take a Luke?"

"Or wipe its Bruno," Luke said.

"I thought that by seventy years old I'd be shut of smart-ass boys."

"What would you do without me?"

"I don't know. Sit the hell down. Maybe even sell my tools and start scratching lottery tickets."

Luke studied his cigarette without blinking. He waited a second before looking up with bleary eyes.

"He'll turn up," Bruno said. "You know."

"I let him in my father's bed and lay there afraid to move."

Bruno waved him away, then patted his thigh.

"Dry up now," he said.

He came out of the fields driving slowly along the wet gravel of the quarry road and went up a hillside where he could see the country to the south, flat woodland thick with oak and slanting birches. Off beyond the trees was the swollen brown current of the Watega River. There were two bulldozers parked upon flatbed trailers and a metal toolshed erected on a makeshift foundation of cinderblocks. Firebreaks were cleared to either side of the road and a few birch trunks lay like bones in the mud. He knew that after a good freeze they would burn these trees and bring the charred land to grade so they could dig the footings for what the newspaper claimed would be the biggest dealership for boats and motor homes in Central Illinois. The old man cursed to himself and shut down the truck.

"You got permission to cut down here?" Luke asked.

"This time next year," the old man said, "Ed Johnson will be selling lawyer's boats right where we're parked. Them bulldozers will shit up the last stretch of good woods in the county. All so those rich bastards can make a mess of the river and their wives can stuff themselves into bikinis. It ain't going to be pretty come summer. You ever see a woman wearing a bikini that shouldn't?"

"I ain't never seen one that should," Luke said.

"You just haven't learned to look yet. Some of them are what I call foolers."

"Foolers?"

"Yessir," Bruno said. "Catholic girls who wear baggy dresses. You got to practice looking real fast when the wind blows the skirt around their thighs."

"They'll scream murder if they catch you."

"If you're gawking like a drunk pervert. But if you just look real fast, they'll smile, almost thanking you for having such good taste. I ain't never met a woman who didn't like a compliment."

Bruno and Luke sat smoking a while before the boy got out. A long rolling tear went through the overcast sky to the north and from it fell vague daylight. He emptied the thermos into the canteen cup, then stepped outside into the weeds, sinking past his bootheels.

Luke stood on the bumper hitch taking up the two axes. His jean cuffs were already dark with mud. From the wet fields came a wind and all through the wood the birch branches beat together as if a room filling with applause. Bruno leaned against the truck hood and sipped coffee. He turned up his mackinaw collar and remembered when this forest ran for ten miles with the river course. It was a long time ago. He saw his father again halting the mules that pulled the heavy oak trunks off the river bank, telling young Bruno that here was Poland in the way of these muddy woods, before he raised the whip and beat the mules toward the quarry road and the saw mill in Charbonneau. That was all he knew of his father, this blue-eyed Pole from the Silesian forests who spoke only fifty words of English, his hands made raw and scaled from scoring stone from the quarry walls, his face forever sallow from the mustard gas that scorched his lungs in the Muese-Aragonne. Bruno's cigarette burned down and seared his knuckles and he pitched the butt. Luke came along the truck laughing, the two ax heads blade down over his shoulder.

"Sometimes I'd like to know where the hell you go," Luke said.

Bruno sucked the burn on his knuckles. The wind smelled of snow. He reached in his pocket and took out a pair of leather gloves and handed them to Luke.

"I don't need them," Luke said.

"Your hands are like a baby's ass," Bruno said. "You'll be bleeding after ten minutes with an ax handle."

"I need to get them toughed up for the Marine Corps."

"What do I have to do to get you off that?"

"I have to take my turn."

"Boy, I'd rather see you run off with the carnival. Or just drink whiskey and lay up in the weeds with high school girls."

They walked along the thicket of scrub oak and brown brier and soon the Watega River was in sight, flooded back into the bankside trees. The current was slow and murky, partly a skein of dead leaves. Bruno squatted at the river's edge and took up a green leaf while Luke stood amongst the birch trees as if trying to figure which three the old man would fall.

"Which ones you want?" Bruno asked.

Luke leaned the axes against a stump stripped of moss by the rains. He pointed out two solid birches close to the flood crest. The old man stood with the help of a hickory stick he found amongst the flotsam.

"They ain't a good choice," he said.

Luke studied the width of their trunks.

"They're fine trees," the old man said. "But I ain't going to drop them. You know why?"

"No."

"They are growing on the downside of the slope and them trunks are only a yard away from the waterline. Which way they going to fall?"

"Into the water."

"What three would you take now?" the old man asked.

Luke pointed out three birches at the end of the copse. The wind came very cold down the river and blew his bangs in his face. The old man let the green leaf fall from his hand.

"Yessir," he said. "They'll fall back into the clearing. Come on, boy, we're burning daylight."

They set to work with the axes, and the blades hit the white wood one after the other and birch quavered from crown to trunk. The tree fell and lay heavily upon the tan weeds. A blister had already formed on Luke's palm and it was the size of a cigar butt. The skin was white and broken, the water dripping down his wrist. Bruno looked at the boy's hand and then looked at a sparrow's nest unraveled in a puddle.

"You ain't going to have no skin on those shithooks," he said.

"A hook's made of metal," Luke said.

"OK," the old man said. "You ain't going to have no skin on those dick-skinners. Remember them hands is your best girl. Rosie Palms."

"It's been a sin to laugh at that since 1939," Luke said.

Bruno reached in his pocket and tossed Luke the gloves. The boy let them land by his boots and gave back a toothy grin before spitting into his palms and rubbing them together. He took up the ax again and soon they fell into the rhythm of chopping down the next birch. The wood chips dropped stark and white upon the mud. The tree fell and then came the next until they all lay with their branches fused together.

The sky darkened when the old man turned to strip the

limbs from the trunks. Luke let the ax fall away and stood staring at his palms. The old man saw blood on the ax handle, then let go a hard sigh.

"Go over to the creek and wash your hands," he said.

Luke was trying to light a cigarette with bloody fingers.

"Drop the goddamn Marlboro and go clean your hands," Bruno said. "Keep them under where the water comes over the rocks."

"I can do it and smoke."

"Why are you still mouthing me?"

Luke shook his hands so that the blood splattered on the fell leaves, a sound not unlike rain. He pushed up his jacket sleeves and walked to the creek, then sat on a stump and let his arms dangle far away from where the old man told him to go. Bruno shook his head and rolled a cigarette. He smoked while the river spooled past with foamy scuz and deadwood.

The oak was down and stripped of its branches, the limbs strewn and cockeyed over the weeds. Grandpa's white hair was undone by the wind and blown across his crowlike face. Bruno stood beside him, shawled by a blanket. The two of them gathered about the stump of the fell tree. His father knelt by the frozen river and hugged a birch where he coughed up gas from the Muese-Aragonne until his black beard dripped blood. His eyes were dark, his broad shoulders tremored in violent fits. Grandpa lit his pipe and stood still like a bird. Bruno looked away from his father when a young buck ran through the birches along the slope. The deer loped fuming cold breath and ran a wide half moon over the fell oak and through the heaped branches and passed by his father loosing lung to the bank mud and cursing God in a language not his own. It ran out upon the Watega frozen into wavelets and the ice opened like a sinkhole. The buck twisted and bobbed, its small antlers thrashing against the ice, death coming suddenly as if it were planned.

Grandpa had his pipe drawing well when Bruno came forward to see. His father was retching dryly now, the wind coming

with sleet. Bruno followed the hoof prints in the snow off the
bank and out to the hole so many times his eyes blurred. The
sleet disappeared into the hole and the water from its thrashing
had sleeved black upon the snow. He cried because he knew the
buck was dead beneath the ice, but he could not look away from
the hole. He closed his eyes and imagined one hundred deer lop-
ing across the snow and ice with eyes like new stars, flying far
above the earth, skylighted by moonlit clouds, their shadows
cast upon the ice in slow drift. He promised these phantoms that
one day he would follow them until their flying ceased, over
mountain and river, but his following would be done afoot, for-
ever afoot.

The old man's cigarette burned down and singed his
knuckle hair. He took the last draw and stove it out with his
boot toe. Luke's soft brown eyes were looking into his. The
boy's hands were wrapped in white socks and he tried grip-
ping the ax handle, but his fingers would not close.

"Where were you?" Luke asked. "I was standing here
more than two minutes before you saw me."

"What do you got on your feet?" Bruno said.

"Just my boots now. I'm ready to clean up them trunks."

Bruno shook his head. He turned up his mackinaw collar
and reached for the tobacco sack and papers. The blood from
Luke's hands had already soaked through his socks.

"Come one, boy," he said. "Let's go before the snow."

"What about these trees?"

"I don't want to get stuck down here with the snow that's
coming."

Luke eyed the clouds as if to find evidence of this snow.
Bruno took the axes and walked slowly up the slope. The boy
followed and they did not speak. There were three oaks along
the creek that the young bucks had scratched and gored with
their antlers. The bark peelings lay where the roots jutted
from the mud and hoof prints went the very way of their
walking. The old man thought to show Luke, stop and just let
him see, but he did not and only walked on with his eyes peering steadily from under his cap brim.

Through the glass doors Luke saw that the bowling alley was empty before he went inside. The carpet was bald and gum-stained. An old woman with button-black eyes sat behind the shoe-rental desk, turning the pages of a movie magazine. She vaguely watched the idiot boy sweep the lanes with a dust mop wider than his legs were long, himself pear-shaped and laughing at nothing while he trod down the wooden straights as if climbing stairs. His chin shined drool, his tongue hung thick and white over his bottom lip. Luke heard pool balls breaking and dropping in pockets around the corner. He walked toward the sound.

His father sat alone at the bar and drank beer from a bagged six-pack. He saw Luke coming in the barback mirror, his eyes red and soapy amongst the rowed necks of liqour bottles. He grinned and popped a beer tab, then pushed back the stool next to him. In the pool room, a Mexican kid picked up his cigarette from the table edge and drew smoke and looked at Luke as if he could not see. Luke walked slowly forward but did not sit down.

"Suit your goddamned self," his father said.

He drank from the beer, his lips scabby and swollen.

"You been fighting?" Luke asked.

"You ever know a day when you ain't?"

"Come on," Luke said. "Let's go home."

His father waved him away. There was only the ribald laughter of the idiot, a pool ball rolling slowly through the gutter.

"It's been four days," Luke said. "I've been walking around looking for you in the rain."

"Damned if I shouldn't rent your ass to the county sheriff so you can hunt down fugitives."

"Your car's the only one left in the lot."

"Where's the other hound?" his father said.

"Grandpa ain't here," Luke said. "It's just me."

"Bruno fucking Konick. Now there's one son of a bitch that can hunt in the rain. Some say he got his Distinguished Service Cross by sneaking up on German snipers on his belly when it was storming one night. K-Bar in his teeth and killing them up close. Problem was he couldn't do nothing but shake his head after he snuck up on me. Then he got tired of what he kept finding. It dawned on him to stop looking like it should dawn on you."

"I just want you to come home," Luke said.

"You know what that son of a bitch said to me after I got my Purple Heart? He looks right at my scarred face and says, 'A Purple Heart only means you can get shot.' I was sitting in the hospital up there at Great Lakes and the war hero says that right to me. Fuck him."

His father's eyeballs sagged in his head before his eyelids half closed. In the pool room, the Mexican kid set the balls into the triangle to continue playing alone. Luke came forward to touch his father, his denim jacket stained from rain and sour beer, but he could not.

"Let's get you home before the rain starts again."

His father's head swayed. He lit a cigarette and set it to drool smoke in the ashtray.

"Maybe the bitch and Larry Stewart will be there to give us a show," he said. "There's men who'd just as soon watch and whip their skippy than anything else. You know something about that?"

"I never watched them."

"You weren't in a hurry to run his ass out of my house."

Luke was silent. He did not know what to do with his hands.

"Just get out of here with your goddamned wet eyes," his father said.

"This ain't you."

His father tried slapping two empty beer cans off the bar but missed them both. He fell upon his shoulder.

"Who do you think you're hearing?" he said.

Luke turned and walked off with bleary eyes. The idiot stood in the lane he'd just swept and held the mop high, shaking the dust from the long red head. He laughed big laughs while the motes fell and powdered his black hair. He tried catching the fuzz with his tongue the way a child does snowflakes. The old lady who rented shoes shook her head and did word-finds with a grease pencil used to keep bowling scores. Luke went out into the night. The first gestures of a cold wind stung his eyes and shook the powerlines where they ran sagging from pole to pole.

The sun was barely visible now, a dirty mute globe, the sky awash in a fog of snow. The old man took a deer trail that led off the river bank, up along a craggy draw where ice made thinly about the jagged limestone, the ax stuck out before him to push away limber scrub branches. He came out of the thicket and stood atop a hill lined with pines and looked out at the birch forest. The bulldozers were parked upon the flatbed trailer. The snow sleeved the firebreaks the workmen cleared, white rags upon black ground. The interstate ran beyond. He squinted his eyes against the wind and imagined the fire. The birches burned as if hundreds of men bound at stakes, all to make room for the dealership that would sell motor homes and pop-up campers and jet boats.

It was this birch forest he conjured the day he turned away from the gray men in the wire at Dachau. The survivors pressed against the razor barbs, crowding toothless and diarrhea-soaked, though the gate was open, the towers without guards or machine guns. He looked at his soldiers before he left for the birches, the sloweyed farmboys from the Dakotas, the decorated wops from city streets, the ruins of the squad he led off the LST at Omaha Beach where they crawled through surf like red wine, tasting salt and the blood of strangers, the heads still strapped into steel pots floating past. He saw no difference between the gray men and the men the war had made his soldiers. The squad was one man now, cloned, cast of a type with muddy beards, torn wool pants, the metal spoon in every field-jacket pocket, tied off to a button hole from a lanyard made by a bootlace. Their faces were so drawn that for a moment he forgot their names and gave up hope of ever remembering them.

He slung his rifle over the arm wet with Wilburn's lung blood and walked away. A full company of infantry was before the wire now, the tanks marring the spring grass beside the road. The soldiers held rags over their faces like bandits, some vomiting into cupped hands from the stench. The gray men murmured prayers for the dead where the bodies lay in the mud with eyes so wide open that no man could tell who was alive. He closed his eyes and vanished off into the ranks like he followed the deer that had crossed his squad's line. The birches rose from memory, quiet in a winter night, the paper bark and the snow fusing together until they were one color. He and the deer loped off like brothers. The herd was coming back from foraging in the fields and the bucks hurried the spotted yearlings and does, and the yearlings and does moved like dreams through the snowcover and bounded and glided beautifully and their eyes were aglow with amber shades. The young bucks twisted and dueled with their small racks. They moved down into the white forest and went deep into the trees. He and the young deer followed, heading off where the stars meet the horizon.

The lieutenant took the handkerchief from his nose and mouth, his young face a mosaic of dirt and freckles. His soft hazel eyes were welled with tears. He stood flanked by two dumbstruck medics, the three of them beside the Sherman tank that idled in the camp gate. The lieutenant twitched and blinked, glancing off into the wet corpse piles as if trying to find his bearings in a storm. The cloned soldiers passed like fog while he called to them, but none would lift their eyes. He ordered them to make stretchers from their ponchos. The two medics eyed their boots. The soldiers paid him no mind and went forward to hunt for stray SS, prepare for a counterattack.

The lieutenant grabbed this sergeant of infantry who passed through snow-lined birches with deer. He turned and fumed cold breath and shook himself free. He was an antlered buck now and not a soldier at all.

"Sergeant," the lieutenant said, "you get your squad together and make stretchers from your ponchos. You do it quickly."

"I ain't no sergeant," he said. "I love does. I forage down into the snow banks for field corn. I follow the rivers and sniff the wind for coyotes and hunters."

They locked eyes while the rain flecked the faces of the gray men in the wire. When the lieutenant repeated his order, the sergeant shoved his rifle hard into the officer's ribs so that the gunsight was lost in the folds of his field jacket.

"I've seen worse," he said. "Felt it, too."

The old man could not remember what happened next. There was a moment when he and the boy lieutenant stood amid the chaos of liberation, where men cloned by killing met men cloned by hunger, but the lieutenant was soon gone with the medics, and he walked off with the herd, not a deserter, not an AWOL, but a deer with his brothers, loping off into the birches to bed down for the night. If the MPs arrested him, he could not say, but through the corpse piles the soldiers roamed and the old man guessed he had roamed with them, because later he was riding upon a Sherman tank with the ruins of his squad, pressing toward the Elbe River.

The image of the coroner caught in the wax floor blurred before resolving when the morgue lights flickered from the ice storm, then again when Bruno Konick blinked from nerves. The examining table where Bruce lay dead beneath the white sheet appeared upside down in the tiles. The body was not yet thawed from spending three nights beneath leaves in the ditch ice along the quarry road. Bruno took off his baseball cap and came slowly forward.

The coroner was a fat man who breathed loudly through his nose. When he lifted the sheet, Bruno saw the two of them reflected in the floor like people from a sepia print: himself holding his hat, the coroner squeezing a handful of sheet. The ice came hard against the windows of the whitelit examining room. The coroner shifted his weight between his feet. Bruno twisted his cap bill into strange shapes.

"The deputy told me some deer hunters found him," Bruno said.

"They came across him at about four o'clock this morning," the coroner said.

"They was out poaching."

"I guess. First shotgun weekend is after Thanksgiving."

"They sure the hell were out poaching," Bruno said. "I hope there wasn't no boys with them."

"You'd have to ask the deputy that. All I have is their names on the report. It doesn't say anything about their ages."

"I just hope they was all men who might have seen worse. A boy wouldn't know what to do with this."

The gray hair the coroner combed over his bald head was slick with tonic. He coughed without covering his mouth. Bruno eyed his wet boot toes.

"The deputy say if he was going to do anything about them poaching?" he asked. "They'll shoot yearlings. They don't care."

"All you got to do is glance and nod, Bruno," the coroner said. "I know it's him but it's something we got to do."

The coroner stared at the cinderblock wall like he saw through it. Bruno looked at the cap bill he ruined and tried pressing it flat between his palms. He brushed the ice off his mackinaw sleeve before he looked at the good side of Bruce's face with one blue eye wide open. The thawing blood dripped onto the tightness of the white paper. The head was half blown away from double-ought buckshot and the neck needed a shave. Bruno looked at the cuts and the scars across Bruce's knuckles from getting drunk these fifteen years and smashing any glass that held his reflection. His eyes bleared so he turned and nodded that it was time to pull back the sheet.

"You want some time alone with him?" the coroner said.

"Would you?"

Bruno stiffened when the coroner touched his shoulder. He nodded his thanks to the man and walked from the examining room with his cap in his hand. Outside, the wind rushed the ice across the small parking lot.

He and Len came into Saint Marie's Cemetery after a night of hard winds, past the wrought-iron gate, the block crypt where the parish laid the dead priests. A gel of slate clouds veiled the pines on the sandhill to the west and behind the overcast the twilight came cold. Len was too small for his age, just turning twelve, and the two lanterns he carried pulled straight his thin arms. Bruno took the pick and shovel off his shoulder while two crows flew from a headstone and circled the cemetery. He looked at his son where he stood watching the birds as if lost beneath the clouds. He started to call him, but only turned, walking for the site beyond the thin oaks where Father Devareaux wanted the grave dug by morning. His wife lay past the limestone grotto for Saint Marie. She was dead eight years now, her name covered with corn-chaff, but he would never look to know.

There was no time to drive the stakes and mark the grave with string so the length and width would measure uniformly. He started too late in the day, and his digging would continue past dusk by lanterns. Bruce ran off sometime in the morning dark, climbing out the window in gusts that knocked fenceposts from the ground, warped the barbed wire. By dawn, the winds lulled enough for Bruno to go out looking and he went alone through the ruined fields, down along Dog Creek where he came upon two bucks dueling over their warring reflections in the water. They slashed with sharp antlers until their racks locked and they reared back upon wet haunches, straining their necks to free themselves. They fought with bulged throats before going still, each buck stressing its eyes to see the other while the splash lines vanished from the creek. Bruno stood watching, hypnotized by their quivering hinds, until the deer collapsed from exhaustion. Only then did he remember that Bruce was gone and he had a grave to dig.

Bruno laid the shovel between the two headstones while Len wandered the cemetery with the lanterns dangling from both hands. He thought to call the boy, but left him alone watching after the crows, nearly shuddering when Len passed by a tree and was shown small by comparison. Bruno kicked away the dead leaves until there was a rectangle of grass, then heaved the pick into the ground with hard, overhead swings, goring two lines long, two lines across. A shower of dirt fell down his coat collar. He stopped and pulled a root from his shirt, then patted the Luger pistol shoved into his belt. The old German schoolmaster had given it to him as a gesture of sur-render when the war was almost over. The man was no soldier and introduced himself as a professor of Latin and geometry, speaking English in the way of British officers. His eyebrows were singed away, his eyes strained to see without glasses. He'd walked from the burning church that tinted the River Elbe orange, his Whermacht tunic missing buttons as if issued to him off the back of a corpse. He held the Luger by the bar-rel and presented it to Sergeant Bruno Konick while the last of his boy students sank into the river with the Iron Cross around their necks.

The Luger then sat thirteen years in a shoebox hidden beneath a loose floorboard until Bruce found the pistol and the ammunition it fired. He taught himself to load and shoot, then moved across the country for three nights as if an archangel. He trespassed upon farms and shot chickens point blank through the wire of their coops, executed pigs where they rooted in the thawing mud, even broke into Andy Janick's barn and shot a horse in the ear. He woke Len before dawn and described for him the dying of the animals until Len sweat cold. Bruno found out and tied Bruce to the clothesline and beat him with a belt buckle. The boy only laughed, his eyes dilated as if orgasmic, and was gone by first light.

The mortar rounds fired from the north bank of the Elbe burst the water made orange by the burning church and sent wavelets over the few boys still floating. The engineers stood chest deep in the glowing water and bolted together a pontoon bridge with long wrenches.

"We was fighting these little boys?" Bruno asked the school-master.

70

*"Their recitations of Virgil were very poor this term," he
said. "Many have not yet learned the patience."*

"I don't believe it."

*"They are hanging boys who will not fight. You will see them
swinging from lampposts. From beech trees. You will see them
very soon. My boys were given the Iron Cross for the heroes they
were to become. The SS carries pocketfuls for the boys."*

"Why didn't you surrender?"

"My own boys would have shot me."

*"You ordered them little boys out into the open for us to kill
them? Is that what the hell you did?"*

"Sergeant, I am no soldier."

The crow circled the cemetery before turning overland for
the sandhills. Len walked up behind Bruno. His eyes were wet
from the cold.

"You don't have to hold them lanterns until it's dark," Bruno
told Len.

The boy's eyes were like bad glass.

"Bruce will turn up," Bruno said. "We'll just wait until he's
hungry and set out a bowl."

Len was silent.

"It's them dead animals, ain't it?" Bruno said.

"Yessir."

"He'll work it off for them farmers. I'll see if I can make a deal
with the sheriff so he don't got to go away."

"He put the gun to them and shot," Len said. "Right up on
them."

"Drop the lanterns and stand away," Bruno said. "I got to
start this grave."

The boy did not move.

"You got something more to say?" Bruno asked.

"I know what it felt like," Len said. "For that horse. Them
pigs, too."

"You better move back unless you want this pick through
your head."

Len walked off slowly amongst the stones. Bruno spat into his
hands and set a tobacco twist against his cheek, then undid two

71

coat buttons. *His pick mauled the tanned grass and the earth it turned was hard and peat brown, smelling of old rain. The cold ground broke into clods and he swung the pick until the loose dirt swallowed the head. He then took up the shovel and glimpsed the boy swaying in dance near the iron gate. Len cradled his arms against his chest and rocked as if he held an infant. Bruno shoveled and Len sang, humming over the words to a song he did not know, the shrill boy voice tearing holes in the silence. The singing haunted Bruno and he counted aloud each spadeful.*

The first tanks crossed the pontoon bridge while the dying fires let the night become the night. The engineers came laughing from the river with their wrenches, the slung carbines dripping on their backs.

"You will kill many such boys on your way to the Reichstag," **the schoolmaster said. "You will leave the ditches full."**

"You are a son of a bitch."

"Germany will stand to the last boy."

The wind lulled and the singing came across the cemetery like the first raindrops. Bruno pitched the Luger into the grave and patted down the dirt before climbing out. He closed his eyes and stood a while in his own darkness, then opened them and walked without his tools for the gate. He ducked behind the crypt and the dead leaves came over his boots. Len's voice floated between the wind beats. "I love you, yes I do, on a plane, in the rain, riding up to heaven true." The boy danced wide-eyed in the gateway and his small legs cast no shadow. His hips swayed, he rocked upon his feet, all movement in time with his song. The boy turned and Bruno saw that he was caressing a dead tom cat, its limp head also keeping time. **When the fires burned down, the river went black and showed nothing of the boys.**

Bruno Konick chewed a dead cigar butt and drove through town looking for his grandson while the snow came silently. The noon was white as eyes and the snow paled the headlights, pasted the tree trunks. Traffic crept along Grant

Street and many cars slid over the curbs before fishtailing into telephone poles. There were two accidents on the Union Avenue overpass. The drunks came from the VFW Hall without coats to watch the sheriff's men close the street. The blue and amber lights from the squad cars strafed the blowing snow.

The boy stood on the porch steps staring bleakly at the truck when Bruno pulled up the gravel drive. He saw him and the red bungalow only between wiper swaths. Luke wore the field jacket and wet snow disappeared into his face. He climbed into the truck with red eyes and the two of them sat quietly at their ends of the bench seat. Luke rolled down the window and spat hard.

"I've been calling you since seven this morning," the boy said. "I let the phone ring and ring. I figured that maybe you left off on a bender of your own."

"When did you ever know that to be true?" Bruno said.

"I figure he learned it from someone."

The wet snow had pasted Luke's bangs to his forehead. Bruno reached over and gripped his grandson's thigh.

"He's dead," Bruno said. "I identified him in the morgue. Some poachers found him out by the quarry road just before dawn."

"You've known since then?"

"I didn't think there was any reason to tell you right away. You got a whole life to know and now you do."

"There was no reason for me to be alone and guessing it."

"Maybe not."

"No," Luke said. "There sure the hell wasn't."

Bruno drove them away into the slanting snow past the closed steel mill at Hennepin Road, the sky the color of sheet metal, the town slowly fading away into the white fields. Luke was quiet and sat against the truck door like a shadow, tensing whenever Bruno went to touch him. The drifting closed the Illinois Central tracks and a long freight heading north to Chicago was stopped off in the fields.

Luke lit a cigarette and cracked the window.

"He do it himself?" he asked.

"He did."

"He wouldn't have just froze to death. He never got that drunk."

"He got that drunk."

Bruno looked into the boy's eyes, the boy into his.

"I don't think my mom ever forgive him for coming home ugly," Luke said.

"That ain't true."

"The bitch should have loved him more. He was a hero."

"You ain't got no excuse to talk about her that way."

"After what I heard her doing."

"He wouldn't have made it this far if it wasn't for her."

"What's that supposed to mean?" Luke said.

"You just don't say that no more about your mom. And he wasn't no goddamned hero."

"Fuck you," Luke said. "He told me what you did to him when he came home."

Bruno Konick nodded grimly and let it pass, then turned the truck overland, heading into the harsh white way of the country.

That night the old man and Luke sat by pale lamplight at the table and ate a supper of ham and beans. The kitchen was sparse but clean and without a utensil younger than the boy. The chairs were cane-backed. The table was built by the old man himself that first spring after the war when he caught his wife masturbating and moaning a dead man's name. Luke picked at his plate and soon his meal was so cold that the fat congealed white on the ham pieces. He looked out the window as if studying each flake coming down upon the fields. The old man uncapped a bottle of Early Times and filled two glasses to two fingers. Luke waved the drink away with his hand.

"You said something about your mom not loving him," Bruno started. "I want to set that straight right now."

Luke picked up the bourbon and shot it back.

"He never loved her the way she deserved to be loved," Bruno said. "I guess he had some heat once. She came from a family of trash. Hillbillies who wandered north to work the factories during the war. Her father died from the black lung he'd brought up from the coal mines and her mother took to whoring in the Station Street bars after the war. I knew her. Everyone did. Elveta was her name. She'd put your mother and her brother to sleep in the front seat of this Plymouth right in front of the tavern while she brought men out to the backseat. Two-dollar Elveta. Your uncle just run off one day."

"I heard every one of her excuses," Luke said.

"She was so young and beautiful that I thought she'd ease some of the meanness in him. It wasn't Vietnam that did it to him."

"Why do you keep telling me that?" Luke asked.

"Because you ain't listening."

They sat there quiet. The sun yet paled a low rim of sky out west and in the vague light bare trees wound from the white earth. Luke held a cigarette to his lips a long time before lighting it.

"He left the both of you when you were three," Bruno said. "He stayed gone until you were four. He turned up drunk in Detroit and got beaten by some cops pretty bad. I had to go after him. I don't think he would have come back by himself."

Luke watched the band of grainy light along the horizon turn dark.

"It was your mom who wanted me to bring him back," Bruno said. "I didn't want to. I always told my boys that if they end up in jail, they can get themselves out. Sometimes I wish I wouldn't have gone. I wish that for you."

Luke stared at the ham on the end of his fork, then dropped the fork so that it bounced, knocking over the salt-shaker. He thumped the table with his knee when he stood and the cold coffee splashed from the cups. Bruno tossed napkins on the spilled coffee while Luke started back into the room where his father once slept.

The wind punched at the windows. The old man stood up from his chair and put on his mackinaw and went outside. It was done snowing by the time he reached the shed. The winds formed jagged drifts out in the fields and the pale moonlight streaked a fault line in the clouds. The dogs barked upon seeing him and jumped against the chain-link pen, their long hair matted with snow. He raised a hand to quiet them, then looked back at the house where Luke's shape and shadow passed and turned in the yellow window-panes like a shooting-gallery bear. He watched until the boy ceased movement and the window glass went black.

He opened the shed door and lit a lantern and set it by the stone hearth. The walls appeared out of the darkness, papered with faded newsprint and old girlie calendars from trucking companies. The tools were hung in rows, attended by their shadows, so many now that he knew not what he had. He lay twigs and four birch logs in the hearth and lit them and went outside with a charred coffee pot and brought it back filled with snow and left it by the fire.

He took the lantern over to the workbench and set it on the shelf beside a new whiskey bottle. The Whizzer frame was upright in the two vises and he watched its shadow contort against the wall. He tested the sandpaper's grit on his wrist, then rubbed the frame with long, even strokes. The rust and the crud powdered away and the bare metal appeared on the crossbar. He brushed it off and his hand turned red. The metal was shineless, pitted and dry, colored like shale. He smiled and took up some new sandpaper, folding it three ways. Soon the whole frame would be bare, the rust and paint layers gone as if they had never been at all. He might paint this Whizzer the red of firetrucks, but he had a week to decide what it once truly looked like, maybe even longer.

Len held the prostitute's back to his chest under the wool blankets and ran his hand over her stomach and imagined her small body had warmed while he kissed her neck. She looked out at the snow without expression, a wet snow leaning through the city lights. He brought his leg over her thigh and touched her hair, ears, the soft undersides of her breasts. She rolled to her back and closed her eyes and let him enter her. The snow was shadowed across her face. He made this prostitute someone else, a woman he had never known, and imagined eyes that lilted with her breath, warm legs locked about his waist. When he finished, she rolled to her side and lay as before, scarred by the snow shadows. The only sound was the clanking of the steam radiator across the room. He looked at the cracks in the ceiling.

"I came to Chicago in the summer of 1970 and worked

what jobs they would give me," Len said. "I washed dishes in a South Loop cafeteria with Afroed blacks. I pulled draughts in the taverns beneath the dark girders of the Lake Street El. I was in exile from the ways of my father, and shot dope into my arms until there were no veins left, then found more in my legs. I believed I was hurting him for the way he refused to imagine what Bruce had done to me. My father is a man who hates that he cannot stop remembering. He would become a rock if he had his wish. I lied to myself about hurting him. You cannot smoke a rock. You cannot hold fog in the palm of your hand. All I did was follow my addiction through the bars and cab stands of the West Side, always knowing that my father was figuring out ways to forget me.

"My addiction ended one night on the Ashland Avenue bus as quietly as it had begun. Across the aisle sat this young woman who was too fat for her short skirt. Her cheek rested on the seat back and her eyes bounced over potholes with the bus. Semen gummed together the strands of her hair. I guessed some man had talked her into his car from a nightclub dance floor, then dumped her when he was done. They say fat girls will do anything. She was looking at me, this girl wanting so much to be beautiful. I was a junkie but I could not handle her sadness. Sad people must remain invisible. I understood then that my addiction meant nothing to the world as long as I did not steal their television sets to get high."

Len heard fast bootfalls in the hallway one second before a small sledge broke open the door. Two men came inside like dogs cut from their leashes. They were dressed in layers of filthy denim, their hands marbled with dirt. The prostitute was up from the bed and dressing quickly, zipping the white leather jacket over her bare breasts. One man held a .25 automatic, small in his hand, and kept a bead drawn on Len. The girl went to the doorway and looked both ways as if crossing the street. The man with the hammer went through the pile of dirty jeans, the one cupboard. Soup cans fell from the shelves and went rolling along the wooden floor. Len went cold when the gunman walked closer to the bed, yelling Spanish at his partner.

"Where is your money?" he said to Len.

"I gave it all to her."

The man smelled of the greasy taquerias along Eighteenth Street. The partner's eyes searched the walls as if another cupboard might appear from the cracked plaster. His boot toes were mended with patches.

"She says you have money all the time," the man said.

Len looked at the girl but she was dark-eyed like bottle glass charred in a burn barrel.

"She comes twice a week," the man said. "I watch her."

"This is all I have," Len said.

The man pistol-whipped him, the gunmetal thumping hard against his jaw. He tasted blood but then lost the taste.

"Where is your money?" the man said.

"She has everything of mine," Len said.

The girl called to the partner in Spanish, then looked hard at the gunman.

"Hit him in the mouth," she said. "Hit him in the mouth and shut him up."

Len closed his eyes before the pistol fell again and kept them shut until there were no sounds at all.

The glass doors of the Greyhound station were broken and covered with a board. Len carried a small bag from the army. He knew by the hot throbbing beneath his eyes that his face was swollen and marred. Footprints made by melting snow smudged the tiles in the terminal and upon the long benches slept two men without homes. They hugged grocery sacks and lay with open mouths and their teeth were gray like spoiled food. Two pimple-faced sailors sat on their seabags by the candy machines and moved their card game off the floor for an old woman to swing her mop. Len steadied himself in the doorway with one hand. The snow fell against his neck.

The ticket clerk leaned against the counter with his face

in his hands. Len walked over and stood before him while the old woman's mop strings caught in the vending machine legs. The clerk looked up but was umoved by Len's ruined face, as if the disfigurement equaled the ravages of his age. He sighed and dug a pencil eraser into his ear and took it out to study the wax.

"You got any buses to Watega?" Len asked.

"There's a bus that goes everywhere. Is that in Illinois?"

"Yes," Len said. "South of here. Almost straight south."

The clerk laid the pencil by the ashtray. He pecked at a computer keyboard with one finger, deleting and retyping almost four times.

"That spelled the way you'd think?" he said.

Len started spelling Watega, but the clerk waved him quiet.

"That's the Memphis bus," the clerk said.

"I'd guess."

"I ain't asking you a question. You going return?"

Len looked at him.

"Round trip," the clerk said. "You want it for both ways?"

"No," Len said. "One way is all."

Luke and his grandfather followed the hearse out to Saint Marie Cemetery. The old man was quiet and wore a mackinaw over his last dark suit and wended the country roads as if heading toward the river bottom to cut trees. Art Bertrand trailed them in his brown Oldsmobile with Father Stremkowski. It had stormed during the funeral mass and they heard the rains over the organ music melting the snowdrifts until the flat wet plains returned to the grim colors of late autumn. The lightning flashed without thunder in the funeral home windows while Luke stared bleakly at the VA casket where his father would lay forever dressed in the old man's second suit. Only five mourners sat in folding chairs and they were himself and the old man and Art Bertrand and the undertaker Donald Cotter and his boy Bobby with thick glasses. They all helped as pallbearers after the mass. Even the grayed Father Stremkowski with cataracts grabbed a corner of the casket. Luke and the old man walked behind in the rain.

The old man cussed the defroster when they neared the wrought-iron cemetery gates. He wiped the windshield with his hand. Luke zipped his field jacket while the snow lining the hedgetrees vanished.

"I'm surprised not to see more of his friends," the old man said.

"He didn't have any," Luke said.

"I suppose it's a work day."

"You ain't listening. He didn't have any."

"There's Jack Arsenau and Walt Tyne. They joined the marines with him."

The old man steered with both hands, peering off through the smears he'd made on the windshield. Luke watched the exhaust billow from the hearse.

"Will you ever tell me what happened here?" he said.

The old man lowered the window to clear the windshield of smog, but rain spotted on his pant leg.

"I can't see how close I am to the hearse," he said. "I don't want to ram him."

"What the hell made you so quiet?" Luke asked.

"I can't see past the damned hood," the old man said.

"You son of a bitch," Luke said. "All I know is that he was lost and you won't tell me shit."

The old man put his face close to the windshield and rode the brake through the cemetery gates and up the gravel ruts behind the body of his son, the foot of the casket visible in the rain-smeared glass.

That afternoon Luke sat with his grandfather and Art Bertrand at the kitchen table. They drank Early Times over a game of gin rummy. The old men wore white shirts burned brown from the iron and their striped ties were pulled loose and their suit jackets hung from the chairbacks. Art lay down a spread, half the hearts sunfaded from the old man keeping the cards on the window ledge. He unslung his frayed suspenders before penciling his score into the margin of yesterday's newspaper. The old man looked at Art's suit, then checked the numbers he'd written beside a story about county police roadblocks on Route 17 and who the drunks were they caught.

"I always thought you could add better than you could dress," the old man said.

"Kiss my ass, Bruno."

"Just look at him, Luke. Red suspenders with a green striped tie. Vitalis in his hair. He's going to get laid tonight."

"Shit," Art said.

"Ask him how an old man gets a hard-on."

Luke lit a cigarette and studied the rain marring the twilight out west. He'd changed into blue jeans and boots.

"OK," he said, "how does an old man get a hard-on," Luke asked.

Art winked at Bruno before staving his tongue into his cheek.

"What the hell does that mean?" Luke said.

The old men laughed and drank their bourbon in turn. They sat in the soft light from the ceiling lamp. His grandfather poured Art and himself another drink and both men splashed in water from a tin pitcher. Luke laid down the cards and pushed back in his chair.

"The apple don't fall too far from the tree with you cheap Polacks," Art said. "A penny a point ain't stiff enough to fold under."

"I don't have the mind for cards," Luke said.

"You don't need a mind for rummy," Art said. "That's why they call it rummy. Even your granddad can play it."

"Up your ass, Art," the old man said. "I'm the rummy king. Me and my buddy Griffen had a running game all the way from the Kasserine Pass to the Elbe River. We played to a draw on the back of an ammo can the night the Germans quit. Sure as shit. A goddamned draw. Two boys from Arkansas lost a lot of money that night to Donatelli. They had Griffen to win after Normandy but Don knew that nobody was going to win at the end of the war. We'd just be drawed and tired of playing."

"You know what they say about war stories," Art said.

"A drawed rummy game is a whole lot easier to take than you shooting down a Jap Zero with a goddamned bazooka," the old man said. "The backblast would have burned your heels off."

"You know how those things went," Art said.

"I do. After forty years of believing your own lies, they go any way you want them."

"Shit."

Luke looked at the oaks along the lane dripping in the gray light. *What am I going to do?* He lit another cigarette off the one just smoked when the old man dropped a set of keys on the table like he raised the pot.

"I guess his car is yours now," he said. "I can take it away like I give it to you. Take some pride in ownership."

Luke picked up the keys. He said nothing.

"The gas tank is on full and the insurance is paid up until Christmas," the old man said. " I guess you'll need a job if you want to drive it past then."

Art and his grandfather nodded, then picked up their hands and ruminated over the cards. He took the keys and walked out into the rain, then drove away in his father's car with the last cigarettes he smoked snuffed to butts in the ashtray.

He came into town and parked and walked along Station Street. The stoplights bled red and violent on the wet asphalt. He breathed in the small rain that leaned through the darkness. In the taverns the shapes of drinkers hovered at the bars. He came to Bray's Restaurant on Grant Street and stood beside a newspaper machine and watched himself light a cigarette in the glass door. His mother wore a brown waitress uniform and rubbed the back of a man with permed hair and a pockmarked face. They sat close together at the counter. Luke smoked with one boot jacked against the wall before he turned and peered inside again. The cook behind the kitchen window glowed orange from the heat lamp and idly spun the ticket wheel. The dining room was empty except for an old man who ate Swiss steak with a fork. A stained napkin hung from his collar. Luke and his mother met eyes and she smiled. Her mouth moved and the man turned and looked after her and then started to stand with her. She put her hand on his shoulder and the man also smiled and kissed her lips before he sat back down.

You better keep your ass right where it is, you dumb son of a bitch.

His mother hugged herself against the cold when she came outside into the meager rain. Her eyes were swollen from crying. Luke pitched his cigarette into a puddle formed about a crumbled parking block, then sneered at her husband through the window.

"Is that him?" Luke asked.

"His name is Larry," she said.

The old man watched them through the window, chewing with an open mouth.

"I heard him plenty," Luke said. "But I never knew a face to put the moaning on. But now I do. It's a real nice face. Not scarred by anything but maybe zits."

"Why do you have to be this way?" she said.

"I ain't being no way."

She went to hug him, but he pushed her away. He wanted to knock her down into the puddled street. Larry watched from the counter and Luke blew him a kiss.

"I can touch my son," she said.

"I don't know what Larry's been into. He looks like a smooth-talking son of a bitch to me."

"Will you look at me?" she said.

"I ain't here to let you off the hook. I come here to tell you that I'm joining the marines. So with him dead and me gone, you and Larry can go about anywhere in town you like."

"You won't be happy until the last little bit is gone," she said.

"I guess I could tell you what you want to hear," Luke said. "It wouldn't be nothing to me."

His mother started crying and he did not look at her. He walked away from the restaurant where she stood sobbing and soon she was silenced by the cars speeding over the New York Central tracks.

He passed two alleys where rusted burn barrels left stark shadows. He walked to the edge of town and went midway across the Washington Avenue bridge and lit a cigarette and stood smoking it. The town lights bled wandlike on the dark water. The darkness was visible when moonlight fell through the torn clouds, and the rain blew off the scant trees and vanished into the river. He jammed his fists in his pockets and leaned over the railing. *Who told any of them they can just start over?*

Luke heard a car pull up behind him against the curb. The cop was looking at him when he turned from the railing and the squad was parked the wrong way against traffic. He took the radio from his mouth and rolled forward before he stopped again and stuck his head out the window to see. His face was swollen like a stuck blowfish. Cars passed slowly around the squad and drove across the bridge. Luke cupped the cigarette in his hand, out of the wet wind.

"What you smoking there?" the cop said.

"A Marlboro, officer," Luke said. He pulled the pack from his field jacket to show him.

"Don't get smart."

"I'm not smart at all."

The cop studied Luke's face like a man getting ready to throw a punch.

"You know who I am?" the cop asked. "Because I sure as shit know who you are."

"Yessir," Luke said. "Sheriff's deputy Steve LaFrance. You're the man my dad knocked stone cold in Skinny's Tap two years ago. I heard he hit you so hard your tongue fell out of your mouth."

"I'm also the cop who got him sixty days in county."

"You were both drunk the way I heard it," Luke said. "Skinny told my grandpa that you asked my dad when he was going to take his mask off because Halloween was over. He said you wasn't even on duty."

"A cop is always a cop," LaFrance said.

"What do you want with me?"

"I just wanted to make sure you were smoking tobacco."

Luke drug his cigarette like a movie tough and watched himself in the back-seat window. He laughed out loud. The cop sat up and touched his hat brim.

"I see the apple didn't fall too far from the tree," LaFrance said.

"You ain't the first person to tell me that tonight."

"Well," LaFrance said, "I was the one that busted up the tree out of the ice with a fucking pick. His head was blowed off. Sleep on that."

Luke didn't look at LaFrance when he pulled a U-turn on the bridge and drove away, but he saw himself in the back-seat window. He was still standing there in the rear window when the squad sped across the bridge. The puddle water sprayed darkly from the back tires. After a while, he walked back through town to his car. In the cloudy sky he could see the glow of the moon but not the moon itself.

He drove around Watega in the rain, and the empty streets shone with his white headlights. He went down McClellen Avenue past yellowlit house windows and made the curve around Saint Marie's Cemetery with the stones flat in the ground so they could be mowed over, and then along the tracks where a train clicked slow in passing. For a long minute he watched the river high and swift, a grim gray color coursing brutally. He caught glimpses of the river between the boxcars on the railroad siding at General Foods and dreamed himself the water, nothing touching him except the thin wicker shadows of the bankside elms. He parked across the street from the pool hall by River City Liquors where a black rummy waited by the door and grinned like he'd pissed himself.

He walked to the storefront window where inside Adonis Hill played a game of nine-ball against himself. He was short and thin, his arms seeming no thicker than the stick he used to set his shots carefully. Luke waved while Adonis cocked an eye and looked down the cue as if aiming a rifle, then moved over to explore another angle. He had not seen him since their last year at the high school when one day Adonis just stopped coming. The other boys thought him crazy and claimed he sniffed gas from a trash bag and screwed his stepsister.

Luke took a chair in the waiting area off the high school social worker's office. The secretary was away from her desk, though he saw her smiling in pictures with her fat kids, this sad-faced woman who wore floral dresses and a small crucifix. Luke did not notice Adonis Hill until he spoke, leaning forward in his chair with his elbows on the ripped knees of his blue jeans. He looked at Luke, his face already scarred by acne. He said: "Konick, you know something about birds?"

"What kind?" Luke said. "That's like asking if you know something about cars."

"Crows," Adonis said. "The big, mean nigger birds. They can be high in the sky and see a cat and swoop down and stab it with their beaks. You know something about them?"

"I don't think a crow can kill a cat."

"Then you don't know a goddamned thing about them," Adonis said.

"I do. My grandpa lives out in Saint Marie. I watch them all the time, but I ain't never seen one kill a cat."

Adonis sat up in his chair like he'd been waiting all day to talk about crows. There was part of a smile bent at his mouthcorners.

"I'm half crow because I'm half nigger."

"You ain't half shit," Luke said.

"I'd fly far away from the white half if I had me some purple microdot."

"What's that?" Luke asked.

"Shit, Konick. It's acid. Trips. Ain't you ever dropped acid?"

"I've smoked pot before, but I prefer whiskey."

"You're about a country motherfucker, then."

"What does Lareau want to see you about?" Luke said.

"Fucking Lareau don't want nobody to fly. You go see Hanks when you're in trouble. Even Ross the boss Cucio. But when they find out trouble don't scare you, you come see Lareau."

Luke sat back against the white wall, waiting for Adonis to ask him what Lareau wanted with him. Instead, Adonis talked about how he hated small birds, robins and bluejays, because they had small wings and did not spook you when they flew off across cornfields. When Adonis was quiet, Luke said: "My mom left us for another man and my dad just got locked up in county for sixty days because he knocked a cop stone cold."

"Cops are motherfuckers," Adonis said. "But my dad is all crow. He flew far away from the police. He's probably still flying right now."

"Shit," Luke said.

Adonis took a cigarette from his flannel shirt pocket and started cawing like a crow. He tapped the filter and cawed and cawed until Luke thought for sure that he was.

"I ain't never been in trouble in my whole life," Luke said.

"You ain't in trouble, Konick. They only think you might be ready for some."

Luke lit a cigarette and went inside the pool hall. The place was empty except for two country boys playing a slow game at the table by the wall and every second shot was a scratch. They wore western shirts with fake pearl snaps and baseball hats that advertised trucking companies, the bills ruined from folding. They spat tobacco into a shared pop can and looked over at Adonis like they were waiting for him.

Adonis struck the cue ball with the force of his small body, but only two balls broke away from the triangle. One stripe and one solid rolled into pockets. Luke ground his cigarette on the cement floor and bent to study the table.

"You're not supposed to knock in both kinds," he said.

Adonis looked up and the pale light from the hanging lamp fell across his face.

"That ain't something I can prevent," he said.

"My ass, you can't."

"You ever play a full game?" Adonis asked.

"No," Luke said. "But I've watched some damned good players over at the bowling alley. Them guys know where every ball is going to go even before they shoot."

Adonis spat on Luke's cigarette butt and wiped his mouth with his arm. They looked at each other like two housecats while the balls broke on the next table.

"Is it true about your old man out on the quarry road?" Adonis said.

"Who the hell told you?"

"Burton and Drummer."

"How'd they find out?"

"Shit, Konick. Burton's dad sits all day scratching lottery tickets and listening to the police scanner. I think he's too crazy to work."

"So was my old man," Luke said.

"You always told me he was a war hero. A hero ain't crazy."

"I don't know. I lied to myself so much about him that I don't know where the lies start anymore."

"Why you worrying about where the lies start?" Adonis said. "That's like wondering if God's a lady. You ain't never going to know."

"No," Luke said, "lies start when you first tell one."

Adonis shook his head and lay the cue stick across the table.

"You want to help me with something?" he said.

Luke walked around the table and came right up beside Adonis. He smelled of sweat and rain.

"Just back me up," Adonis said. "All you got to do is stand there and keep your mouth shut."

"You got a bottle of something?" Luke asked.

"If you back me up, I'll be close."

"How close?"

"About twenty dollars close."

Adonis led Luke through the pool hall where cigarette burns welted the table edges and smoke rose into the lampshades hanging over the green felt. They went out the back door to the alley, and soon the two country boys stood eyeing them on the wet gravel. Their fists were the size of sledge heads. Luke worried about having to take them in a fight, but the boys only smiled dumbly, as if idiots shown a girlie picture. Adonis called one Rusty and handed him a plastic baggy of oregano. The boys squatted down in the alley. Rusty was buck-toothed and he turned the baggy around in the window light. The friend grinned open-mouthed, and he watched the light hit the bag like a dog charmed by an open flame.

"You like it?" Adonis said.

Rusty sucked his teeth, breathing laughter.

"Ain't one good bud," he said. "But there ain't one stem or seed. Would you look at this? Ain't any at all."

The friend giggled while Rusty shook the oregano in the baggy.

"Looks good," Rusty said. "What did you say this was?"

"Italian green," Adonis said.

Rusty smelled the inside of the bag.

"The shit you say," he said. "Damn. Smells real different."

"The Mafia brings it over," Adonis said. "I get it from a guy in Chicago."

"They a rock band?"

"Yeah."

"Never heard of them," Rusty said.

Adonis rolled his eyes while Luke watched the grayblack night for cops.

"How'd you make out on your last score?" Adonis asked.

"Not worth a fuck," Rusty said. "It tasted like mint and gave Earl here the shits."

Earl pursed his lips and nodded.

"Wouldn't stop the whole next day," he said.

"We bought a bag off some nigger," Rusty said. "Seemed like a good nigger, too. Real polite."

"Didn't you get to hold it?" Adonis said.

"I never thought to ask."

"Well," Adonis said.

Rusty took off his cap, his hair dented from the band.

"You never can tell with a nigger," he said. "Earl here shit in the ditch five times on the way back to Saint Marie. That nigger sure knew what he was doing."

"You got to hand it to them," Adonis said.

"You sure do. But I wasn't the one with my ass in the weeds."

Rusty took two ten-dollar bills from his coat pocket and the exchange with Adonis was made in less than a second. Luke was biting his tongue to keep from laughing when a leashed dog barked from the yard across the alley. A porch light turned on the night.

"Later days and better lays," Rusty said.

The boys ran down the alley in their cowboy boots and hit every puddle.

"Dumb motherfuckers," Adonis said. "Next week I'll sell them parsley."

"No shit," Luke said.

"Them assholes will really think they got something."

They walked across Hobbie Avenue to River City Liquors and Adonis gave the old black sitting outside five dollars to buy them four quarts of Budweiser. He smoked a cigarette rolled in newsprint, his eyes soapy red, and pointed at his mismatched sneakers as if he were telling the shoes something. He rose and reeled toward the glass door, belching profanely.

"Womens like the sweet wine," he said. "But not the bitter beer. Not one taste. But they eat you alive for a reefer."

Luke and Adonis sat on the window ledge and lit cigarettes. The wind blew. They turned up their coat collars.

"How do you know he's coming back?" Luke asked.

"How do you think old Slobo stays drunk?"

"That ain't his name."

"I gave it to him. Don't he look like a Slobo?"

"About as much as you look like an Adonis. I bet you gave yourself that name, too."

"Maybe I did."

"Why the hell would you do that?" Luke said.

"It's a black thing."

"That would be fine if you was even one ounce black."

"How do you know I ain't?"

"Shit," Luke said. "I just think you want to be different from the rest of us."

The old black came back with two bottles of grape Mad Dog and set them on the sidewalk. His eyes ran. The wind twisted his coattails about his legs. He walked off under the viaduct sipping a pint of Chivas Regal.

"What the hell are we going to do with this?" Luke asked.

Adonis shoved the bottles in his coat pockets.

"Get in your car and go find us some girls?" he said.

"You know how to do that?"

"No. I usually wait for them to come around sniffing."

"I wouldn't think they'd sniff a lying sack of shit very long," Luke said.

"You ever been laid, Konick? Not counting fat girls."

"I've been so drunk I almost kissed a nigger," Luke said.

"Up your ass."

They drove around the dark of East Watega and drank the wine, swallowing fast against the sweetness until their necks felt slack and warm. The streets were gouged and craggy beyond the paint factories, lined with paintless clapboard houses, the asphalt strewn with broken glass and things dropped by the people who crossed it that day. Wrecked shoes. Pop cans. A white doll's head done up in minstrel face by the gutter mud. Soaked hamburger bags roosted in weedy back lots like doves. Two kids were stealing lightbulbs from porch lights and shaking the burn from their fingers as if they touched cat shit. Luke looked at Adonis and held the wheel straight.

"You really used to screw your stepsister?" Luke said.

"I ain't got one," Adonis said.

"Why'd people think that?"

"I told them. I even said she had a friend that joined us."

"People thought you were a pervert."

"At least they thought I was something."

"Shit," Luke said.

"No, Konick. My mother left me with my stepfather about ten years ago and he's too numb to be an asshole."

"Where's your dad?"

"I don't know him," Adonis said. "I make up things about him so I got something to remember."

"That's crazy."

"You got to come from something."

"It's still crazy," Luke said.

The wine glazed Adonis's eyes red.

"You do funny things when you know you can't pick your old man out of a crowd," he said.

"You still can't think whatever you want about him," Luke said.

"All I know is that he was a nigger and my mom was a fat white girl with bad teeth," Adonis said. "He probably beat the shit out of her. I bet he hated that she was so ugly."

"That ain't nothing to say."

"You know what kind of white girl goes with a nigger?" Adonis said.

Luke was quiet. He listened to the tires rubbing against the street.

"She was that kind," Adonis said.

"It don't make her bad," Luke said.

"I never said it did. You asked about her. You buried your old man today and you don't hear me asking you no questions. You know why?"

"I don't."

"A mixed motherfucker that lives with his white stepfather gets sick of giving answers. People prod you. But when you go telling them the truth, they always think you're angry."

Luke flipped his cigarette out the window and it went in

a slow red arc. Adonis drank long from the bottle. The wine ran down his chin.

"All I know is that we got to do something," he said.

"We're doing all you can in Watega," Luke said.

"No, Konick. This is just driving around and getting drunk like two pussies."

"You're all talk," Luke said.

"Ain't it always talk?"

"No, Hill. It ain't always talk."

The police car turned the corner off an unlit cross street north of the railroad viaduct and made a U-turn to follow them closely. Adonis shoved the bottles beneath the bench seat. From his rearview mirror, Luke watched the cop talk sideways into the radio when the blue lights began spinning. He stopped the car by the wrought-iron gates of Saint Marie's Cemetery where off among the flat stones the cement crucifix shined in the darkness.

"It's that fat son of a bitch, LaFrance," Luke said.

"Ain't that the cop your dad belted?" Adonis asked.

"Knocked him out and tore him a new asshole in front of everybody."

"Motherfucker," said Adonis.

"You holding anything?"

"No."

"Then just keep your mouth shut," Luke said.

"Motherfuck."

"We ain't killed nobody."

"That don't matter to them."

Adonis pocketed his hands to keep them from shaking. He looked out across the graveyard. Luke heard teeth in his breathing.

The blue lights strafed the wet oaks along the cemetery fence. LaFrance stepped from the squad car and unsnapped his holster. Luke rolled down the window and the cop looked inside, a fat red face with razor cuts and two chins. He shined a maglight in their eyes.

"Where you been, Konick?" LaFrance said.

Luke looked at the greenlit speedometer and blew cold.

"Driving," he said.

LaFrance pointed the maglight at Adonis.

"Where's he live?" he said.

"The trailercourt," Adonis said.

"Did I ask you anything, Flash?"

"No."

LaFrance nodded. He chewed. He put his hands on his hips and looked out at the night.

"Where you been, Konick?"

Luke was silent.

"I ain't going to ask you another time," LaFrance said.

"I was giving Flash here the dick," Luke said.

LaFrance stepped back and took his baton from his belt.

"You both smell like a splib fishing trip," he said. "I want you to step your happy asses out of the car. Konick after Flash, and walk around to my side and put your hands on the hood here."

The cop showed them where with the baton.

"Shit," Luke said. Adonis breathed strangely.

"I told you back on the bridge," LaFrance said.

"No," Luke said. "You just wanted to know what kind of cigarettes I was smoking."

The cop went to open the door, but it was locked. Luke was laughing when he stepped out and LaFrance grabbed him and laid him over the hood and pressed his face sideways on the wet metal with the baton. The cop's breath was metallic from cigarettes. He panted hard and picked up Luke's head by his hair and smashed it against the metal. Luke's eyes swam and the night went darker around him but he was still on his feet. When another set of blue lights sped at them, Adonis Hill went over the cemetery fence and ran off among the stones. The cop stood like a fat man not knowing what to eat first, then cuffed Luke's hands tightly.

* * *

LaFrance held open the squad-car door while another
deputy with sergeant's stripes pulled Luke out by the arm.
They entered the Watega County Jail, a gray building of
cement and grated windows rising above the hickory trees
and the power lines. The cops led Luke down a shiny hallway and through three heavy doors that were buzzed open.
All he saw was the whiteness of the cinderblock walls and
his own shadow upright like his father's the night these
men prodded him through the jailhouse silence with batons.

The sergeant's holstered .38 pulled down his belt and
showed his jockey shorts. He was a thin man with a gut who
struggled to keep his shirt tucked into his pants. They sat
Luke on a long wooden bench and left him handcuffed. The
sergeant leaned on a desk and lit a cigarette and smiled
around it. Luke turned away from his wet, yellow teeth and
studied the bench where the varnish was worn away.
LaFrance grinned and held the nightstick under his arm
like a folded newspaper.

"What do we got here, Steve?" the sergeant said.

"Luke Konick."

"He Bruce's boy?"

LaFrance nodded while the sergeant looked at Luke. His
khaki uniform was wrinkled like cracked glass.

"Your old man spent some of his best nights cuffed right
here on this bench," the sergeant said.

Luke glared and imagined the sergeant on fire.

"He looks like he wants to kill you," LaFrance said.

The sergeant was nodding his head when another deputy
walked down the hallway without stopping.

"Is that you, Billadeau?" he said.

"Yeah."

"Yeah?"

"Yes, Sergeant."

"How long does it take to get hamburgers and coffee?" the
sergeant said.

"How long was I gone?" the voice called back.

"A half hour."

"That's about how long it would take."

"You better get your ass down here with them sandwiches," the sergeant said.

There was no answer, only the sound of bags opening.

"Steve," the sergeant said, "go tell that shit-sack to get his ass in here."

"What about him?" LaFrance said of Luke.

The sergeant walked over to Luke as if a cow limping.

"You want a phone call?" he asked.

"Am I under arrest?" Luke said.

"I asked you if you wanted a phone call."

Luke tilted back his head and gathered up a hocker of phlegm in his throat and spat it into the sergeant's face. The sergeant half-laughed, then slapped him with a flat hand. Luke's neck straightened and went slack. His eyes hazed black and the two cops looking down at him seemed like vague shadows. He was nauseated now, the room lifting up and back, but never going still.

"Goddamn if you ain't a fuck-up, Konick," the sergeant said. "Take him down to three. Make sure he's next to those squirrelly fucking niggers. They need someone to hear them."

"You want me to call Bruno?" LaFrance said.

The sergeant wiped his face off with a shirt sleeve.

"No, goddammit," he said. "He ain't a juvenile."

There was no light in the cell except what fell through the window in the door. Luke sat with his eyes closed and rocked on the metal bunk. The stool was made of the same metal as the bunk and from it came the fetor of a stranger's urine. Somewhere in the jail dark he thought he heard dogs, wind knocking sticks from the river trees, but there was only his own breathing. He rose and kicked at the door with stocking feet and screamed for them to let him out. In the window of the cell across the glowing hallway he saw a black face looking at him and yelling for him to shut his punk ass up.

On a cold morning the old man came out of Hookstra's field with an ax over his shoulder like a tramp's bundle and walked down Leggtown Road. The sun shone white behind the cloud cover. He looked across a field of rotten pumpkins and the birch forest had disappeared with the evidence of its burning, and all the charred branches and smoldering cinders were turned with the black earth. The bulldozers were gone with the flatbed trailers that hauled them. Yesterday, he saw the smoke rising from the trees in violent fits of gray and black, but he did not drive out to watch. He sat on a rock and rolled a cigarette. Two crows glided by searching the ground for what was burned away, their calls sounding close and urgent. The birds scared him. He threw rocks at the air long after they flew west along the river, first seeming themselves, then turning into charcoal sketches.

THE NAMES OF RIVERS

*Without the white trees, there were only the fields and
brown river and the gray sky spread out like a movie screen. He
sat cold upon the rock, studying the cloud welds closely until he
appeared as the sergeant of infantry again, standing upon the
muddy ground of Dachau with his squad. The birch forest and
the deer were gone with his power to imagine he trailed off
among them so far away from the war and the German towns
ruined by the thousand bomber raids where only crows and dogs
lived in the rubble and the people carved steaks from the hinds
of shrapnel-killed horses. There were woodframe barracks
ordered about the parade ground where he stood smoking, and
the gray men who still walked came from them with pick axes
and shovels and sharpened boards. The wind was cold and
brown water stood in the tank tracks. The gray men had already
killed a gypsy kapo, turning his face bones to powder with chair-
legs. His wrecked body lay in the mud among the corpse piles.
They fought over his boots like alley cats.*

*His men brought him a bleeding SS who was badly cut from
the razor wire through which he'd tried escaping. Bruno exhaled
cigarette smoke and watched it drift into the rain. The SS mut-
tered in French and heavily accented German. His face was the
color of a deep bruise and he did not look at the soldiers pulling
him by the arms. Only one jack boot was on his foot, the other
perhaps still in the guard's barracks where the coffee pots
steamed on the stove. He was naked from the waist and blood
streamed from the deep cuts on his legs and his black trousers
hung shredded in the wire where the soldiers had pulled him free.*

*Bruno pitched his cigarette into the mud. The soldiers held
the SS to his feet, though his knees quaked and he coughed wet.
Bruno took the SS's face and forced him to meet his eyes, but the
man only pissed himself. His legs were absurdly white. Bruno
laughed and patted the man's cheek, then took his bayonet from
its scabbard and stepped four paces back, counting them loudly.
He raised the bayonet as if it were a sword, and when he
dropped it, like he'd seen in so many movies, the soldiers fired
their rifles. The reports were without echo. The SS collapsed
upon his back and his legs twisted wrong at his knees. The gray*

100

men danced from true joy, many faces regaining color as if buds coming from winter trees. The healthiest ran forward with the picks and shovels of their forced labor. Bruno stayed them with his hand, and then by firing his rifle once into the air.

The SS reeled in shock and the soldiers held his face straight and forced open his eyes with bayonet tips. Bruno blew him a kiss, then hushed the SS's moaning with a finger across his own lips. They gray men chanted as if aboriginal. Bruno smiled grotesquely while the SS came from shock and screamed, reaching up to the soldiers who had shot out his knees. Bruno then pointed to a small man in the crowd and he moved forward. The soldiers winked at him for he was not a man at all but a boy, enduring puberty without having brushed his teeth or washed his face. The SS reeled upon his back and tried vainly to hold together his knees. Bruno handed the boy a bayonet and the boy nodded with love and straddled the chest of the SS with his bony knees. He stabbed his face, the cheeks, each eye socket in turn. The soldiers fired shots in the air to stay the gray men while the boy wrapped both hands around the bayonet, stabbing until he killed the SS many times over.

The Greyhound bus left Len at the station before the dawn paled the eastern skies over Watega. He walked the curbless street into town while the wind dried the rain on the store-front windows. Two crows landed on the pumps at the Clark Station after the gas truck finished filling the tanks and pulled away. When the birds flapped off and passed low over the sagged powerlines, he looked away from their flight and did not breathe right until they were gone.

The only diner open was a black one named the Viceroy and he ordered eggs scrambled with ham from a mutton-faced woman. She wore a pink housecoat and slippers col-ored the gray of dust and walked by sliding her soles flatly across the brown tiles. The booths near the window were orange and the three tables were made level by sugar pack-ets and folded napkins set beneath the legs. The woman scrambled the eggs in a small kitchen behind the counter and listened to a tape recording from a church service; the preacher ranted about how everything was for the children, the true lambs of God.

The woman brought him his plate. He pushed the ashtray aside and pointed to his coffee cup. She watched him smoke and studied the bruises on his face. He was the lone customer.

"You be grinding your teeth if you have any more," she said. "Coffee same as junk in the Lord's eyes."

"Please," Len said.

She rolled her eyes and came back with an old perk pot. Her head was wrapped around with a floral cloth.

"Thank you," he said.

Len brought the cup to his swollen lips. The steam rose from his plate of eggs.

"It'll scald you good," she said.

The woman drug her feet back to the kitchen and soon sang along with the taped choir by humming deeply from her throat. Not quite a moan, not quite a melody.

He ate and left the diner and crossed the Washington Avenue bridge where beneath flowed the Watega River high from rain and snow. The brown water carried off deadwood and shoots of grass. Men free from the midnight shifts at General Foods and Gould Foundry passed in dented cars and parked before taverns and walked grimly inside the painted-glass doors to drink draught beers in two swallows. The sun came harsh after first light and burnished in the wet streets like treasure. He stood staring into the river until the factory whistles blew and ordered the day shifts to their lines.

All morning he trod the sidewalks for long blocks, down past alley mouths, the traffic lights swinging from wind, the cataracted old men gawking through diner windows. Watega was the way he remembered it. There were the streets of red brick, storefronts without wares, the gas stations where teenaged boys fixed flats to radio songs.

The railroad tracks ran through town and off into the fields as if great braces for the making straight of the earth, and the slow freights passed while trainmen hung from the engine on hold bars and spat into the wind. He walked down Court Street where two black kids searched about the parking meters for dropped change. Their whitewashed hands scratched the leaf mulch from the gutters and they cursed like drunks when they found nothing. Len was run through by a bird shadow when a man spoke to him from an alleyway. He said: "You ain't walking with no place in aim. I know because I've watched you come around five times."

Len stopped and looked up from the rainbow the spilled oil made on the street. The man leaned against the side of a pickup truck and his boots were crossed in the puddle before him. An unlit cigarette butt staved from his mouth.

"There isn't enough town to walk straight in," Len said.

"There ain't enough world for that," said the man.

The gate of the man's truck was down and it displayed his wares. Useless things. Transistor radios without knobs. A baby doll missing an eye and paperback novels moldy from the rain. Odd nuts and bolts and bicycle rims. A hammer taped to its wooden handle. He smiled at Len, showing his black teeth, then lit the cigarette butt with a Zippo lighter that smelled of gasoline.

"Stop a minute and have a look," he said.

"I've seen it all," Len said.

"You ain't hardly studied none of it. I know because I been watching you."

Len pointed at the lighter in the man's pocket.

"You don't fill that with gas," he said.

"Same thing I put in this truck."

Len nodded.

"It ain't all but the same thing," the man said. "I wouldn't have allowed it neither until I tried it myself. Like most things."

Len walked slowly through the puddle and stood a little

away from the man. The morning was too bright to look without first squinting.

"Hot for this time of year," the man said.

Len said that it was. The man smelled vaguely of urine and wet dog.

"You see anything you want to dicker over?" the man asked.

"No."

"I know it. My wares ain't what they once was."

The man scratched absently in the gravel with his boot toe, smiling. He turned his head, looking down the alley, then reached beneath the tarp balled in the truck bed and pulled out a sweaty quart of beer. He poured a plastic cup full. He looked at Len.

"Care for some cold stuff?" he asked.

"No, thanks."

"Go on," the man said. "Get you a snout full."

Len waved it away with his hand.

"I'm sober," he said.

The man drank and wiped his mouth.

"So was I," he said. "Where were you aiming to go in circles?"

"There isn't enough town to walk straight in."

The man combed his stringy gray hair with splayed fingers.

"You said that," he said.

"I did."

"I used to sell real regular to the niggers back when the stores wouldn't let them in on account of them being niggers. I even had me a colored woman and was raising up her kids like my own. None of her people ever minded me because I got them what they needed. Coats and radios and anything they asked for. Even store-bought whiskey. I'd buy my wares from thieves and sell them to the niggers. I was doing real good that way."

"I better get on," Len said.

"The colored preachers even let me set up outside the nigger churches on Sunday. They knew I was doing them a good turn."

The man spat. He looked at his ragged shoes and then at Len who nodded goodbye.

"I killed her," the man said. "I did twenty-five years for it down in Huntsville, Texas, and I'd do it again. She got to where she could go into any store she liked and got uppity—too uppity for a colored woman. There's a line, you know."

"Have a good one," Len said.

"Sure you don't want a bicycle to ride? You could build it up from these parts. Cheaper than buying it all put together."

Len raised his hand goodbye and walked off out of town through the puddles. He hitched a ride in the bed of a pickup truck. The driver was an old man who wore a suit jacket over a red plaid flannel shirt and his wife had a humped back higher than her head. Len sat on the spare tire, his bag between his heels, watching the wind run in the weeds. The road went sunlit and unswerving toward Saint Marie. He banged on the window three miles north of town. The old man stopped and looked at him through the glass with a cocked eye, then glanced at the flooded melon field beyond the barditch. The woman was stiff, her veiny hands folded upon her lap. Len jumped down into the roadside grass and waved goodbye. A flock of starlings came from the horizon to land in the field and peck the rotten melons in the mud.

The ditch water flowed like a rivulet and along the banks of Dog Creek was a sandbag dike filled with gravel. The water was roily and flattened the weeds. Len crossed the bridge where two Mexicans stood by the town sign with a pink hog rooting in the grass. The holes it made in the mud quickly filled with the same water running in the creek. He knew they had walked a long way with the hog by the field mud caked upon their boots. One man yanked a rope tied around the swine's neck while his friend clubbed its hinds with a broken broomstick. The hog was unmoved and only stove its snout deeper into the mud. They looked up at Len and smiled graciously. Their polite expressions did not match the violence they used against the animal.

He followed the road into town past the burned foundation of Cap's Supper Club where the sign still advertised prime rib for six dollars a plate. He nodded down into his coat and lit a cigarette. There were hogs riding in the backseats of sedans and station wagons blooming with dirty-faced children, and one swine eyed Len from a dog cage in a pickup truck. The passing cars had fenders that did not match the hoods, tailpipes tied to the chassis with rags, bumpers attached with twisted coat hangers. Their engines sounded like tin cans drug by string and most left trails of white smoke. He looked back and the Mexicans were kicking the hog, the broomstick broken and floating in the ditch water. The lone farmsteads along the horizon had the solitary look of prisons.

The traffic came along Route One in bursts. He leaned against a breather from the gas main buried underground and watched the procession of junk cars and trucks and the sniffing hogs they hauled. He walked into town and turned down Clay Street where stood a lone sheriff's deputy bathed in the sapphire of his cruiser's twirling lights. His lanky reflection showed in the post office window and he yelled through a bullhorn for the people to stay in their vehicles with the swine. The drunks flowed from Hubert's Bar to see and hid beer cans in open flannel shirts; the most surly among them toasted the deputy with the smiles of perverts. The people paid the cop no mind at all and unloaded the hogs, and they ran squealing into the street, jerking still when they met the rope's end.

Newsprint covered the windows of the old IGA Supermarket. In front was a sign fashioned from a cardboard box that promised the killing and butchering of hogs for fifteen dollars. A young boy waited by the door in a blood-smeared meat jacket. Inside, death squeals sounded before the lone pistol report. The kid was fat and stared vacantly at the daylight as if watching television. His tennis shoes were covered with gore like his pant legs and he took the bills and handfuls of change from the bloated men who muscled the hogs from backseats and truck beds. The drunks mocked the cop and imitated the hogs.

Len went down the sidewalk slowly. An old black sat on the curb and held a young pink pig by headlock. His arms were thin like scrub branches, but he kept hold of the pig while it grunted and rooted in the sidewalk cracks. He looked up at Len, his eyewhites turned yellow, and firmed up his lock around the pig's neck by each hand grabbing a wrist.

"Looks like you got him now," Len said.

"Shit," the man said. "He like a kid almost. Soon as he get tired of rooting here, he going to want to root over there. But people going to be fighting over rooting space before too long."

"You should get you a rope," Len said.

The pig whined and kicked and pulled the man over, but he yanked back.

"The farmer was giving out pigs, not rope," he said. "I didn't think to bring one. I just heard on the radio that there was free pigs and I hitched to the getting place. But the pig shit in the man's car and he threw me out of there."

"Giving away pigs?"

"The farmer probably give away sixty pigs. He say that pork prices got so low that the hogs ain't worth the feed."

"You should get it butchered."

"Hell no. I'm going to keep him. A pig ain't nothing bad to have around. I'm just waiting for enough of them to die off so I can get me a good rope. But some of these white folks won't give a nigger nothing."

"You got a free pig."

"I said *some* of the white folks, not all of them."

"Good luck."

"You going out to Leesville?" the man asked.

"I'm walking same as you."

The man looked down the sidewalk after a pistol shot.

"I sure wish the farmer was giving out dogs," he said.

"Good luck," Len said.

"A free dog would be something to have."

Len headed for the railroad crossing and went along the tracks where the shadows of gray weeds fell over the tracks like loose hairs, and he watched them lie. With twilight came jagged clouds along the northern horizon, and the pink and faded blue light leaked strangely upon the country. He jumped the barditch and stood across the road from the bare hickories that walled the lane running up to his father's house.

There were lengths of cornstalk and fell sticks matting the gravel lane and the tree branches curled and joined overhead so that it was like the entrance to a cave. He walked slowly in this tunnel and came out in the halflight before the whiteboard house that was permanently brown from the field dust. All about lay tractor parts and enormous saw blades oxidized orange and grown over with brown weeds. He moved behind his broken shadow and tried not to think even when the dogs barked from their chain-link pen and he found himself mirrored in the curtainless house windows. He stepped behind a giant hackberry with roots the size of a man's thigh bulging from the earth.

There was a boy across the muddy yard leveling a wrist rocket at the toolshed. He pulled the rubber back past his ear, let go, and the ball bearing slammed against the weathered boards that were once barn siding. The blackbirds scattered off the rail fence. The boy turned and reloaded and sent a determined shot at the darkening sky and yelled after it. He kicked sticks through the puddles. He spat at the wind. His field jacket hung open and flapped about him like wings. Len saw his brother's face sketched so exactly upon him that he felt himself floating.

The knife smelled of tree sap and old blood when Bruce pushed his nose flat with it.

"Sniff it," he told him.

Len drew a cold breath as the rain quit and wind lay the curtains flat along the ceiling. Bruce's eyes shined like bottle glass in dark water and the welts from their father's belt marred his face.

That afternoon, Len had watched their father tie Bruce to the clothesline so he would not run away and then beat him with the belt buckle. He was happy to see it. He wanted him to kill Bruce the way Bruce killed the animals where they stood out of the cold in barn stalls.

"I told you to sniff it," Bruce said.

Len smelled the cold metal. The bedroom walls seemed in motion from the curtain shadows, the quavering tree branches hemmed by moonlight.

"I know you told him about the horse, you little cocksucker," Bruce said. "You better smell it again. Even give it a lick."

Len felt his eyes bouncing. He lay still and near breathless upon the bed. The window was open to the white night. Bruce wore a blanket slung over his shoulders; food weighed down a gunnysack hung by a rope off his back. The knife had a taped handle, something he was sure his brother found, or traded for.

"I saw you watching him beat me," Bruce said. "You was right in the window. You dirty little cocksucker."

Bruce drug the blunt side of the knife alongside Len's nose and then stuck it crosswise into his belt for there was no sheath. He looked down at Len where he trembled as if a branch caught in a storm, smiling to tell him none of this was over. He then climbed out the window into the dark morning of winds with his bundle and set off headlong against them toward the river woods. When the winds came again three nights later, Bruce walked out of the fields with a yearling doe hanging over his shoulders and the blanket was gone. Len watched him lay the spotted deer by the front door while the snow rose about his boots and their father wept and hugged him as of he had stolen no pistol or shot no stock. Len knew that he would be alone.

His eyes were bleary when the boy set the wrist rocket on the car hood. The wind sucked in the weeds. The boy was staring at him where he stood by the hackberry trunk, his hand raised nervously in greeting. Thin clouds came with the wind beats and they drifted across the sky and the quarterdarkness shifted in shade and depth. The boy walked closer, his hands lost in his field-jacket pockets. He studied

Len closely, then yelled for the dogs to quiet themselves, and they did, trembling on haunches and showing yellow teeth slick with drool. Len waited for his father to come up behind him, but he never did. The boy combed his bangs from his face and breathed anxiously.

"My grandpa ain't here," Luke said. "I'd guess he's up at Bertrand's. That's where I'd start looking for him."

"I think your name is Luke," Len said. "Do you know mine?"

The boy looked at him and then his small bag from the army.

"I guess without a truck, you ain't after wood," he said. "But sir, I've never seen you before in my life."

"I know that. I'm your Uncle Len."

Luke looked away twice before he looked off a final time with quivering lips. The cherry trees were black from rain and full of loud birds. The boy was crying and biting his lip.

"You all right?" Len asked.

"There ain't nothing wrong with me."

"Let's go sit a while."

"He's dead, you know," the boy said. "He killed himself with a shotgun out on the quarry road. It's just me and the old man now. I ain't got no sympathy for him, either. He's worse than a fucking lie."

Len went cold and sweat hot and saw the dusk as if through wet glass. He leaned against the hackberry trunk. *It wasn't for you to do that. The forgiveness must be done. I was going to let you do the work and even wait.* After a while Len raised his face and stood straight by the tree where the last bird shadows of the twilight moved across the earth like ghosts and the boy just stood, not looking at him, but looking to him.

Bruno Konick took a stool at the counter inside Bertrand's Café where Art hummed along to big band music playing from the radio while he poured whiskey in their coffee cups and the wind played in the screen-door latch. They sipped the spiked coffee and smoked and looked out at the twilit street where newsprint rolled like tumbleweeds. Miller and O'Brien sat in the window booth and chewed cigars and coughed and scratched lottery tickets with pennies. Bruno poked a spoon from the place setting halfway into Art's stomach. Art looked at him blankly and held the glass coffee pot white with steam.

"Have you gone screwy?" he said.

"Ain't you supposed to let off a giggle when a guy does that to you?" Bruno said.

"Piss on you."

Bruno grinned and set the spoon back between the knife and fork.

"It's a good goddamn thing you ain't out walking around town," he said.

"Why in the hell is that?"

"The river trash might take you for a hog and slow-roast you on a spit. They might even pour beer on your steaming hide."

Art sat the coffee pot on the counter beside an empty donut box.

"I know you must be talking to that pie case," he said.

"I was wondering something," Bruno said. "I know you can't see your toes past that gut, so if you put on a pair of shoes at five in the morning, would you still know which ones you were wearing at noon?"

"Goddammit, Bruno."

"Which are they? Oxfords or loafers?"

"Go to hell."

"You can't remember."

"Shit," Art said.

Bruno sipped his coffee and smiled around the cup rim. Miller and O'Brien were intent upon their lottery scratch-offs and the losers were piled on the table like chicken bones. They wore baseball caps back on their heads and smudged glasses slid to the ends of their noses. Art reached in his pocket and took out two empty packs of Winstons before finding one with a cigarette. He lit it and looked at Bruno and looked out at the street. Bruno put his hat on his knee.

"Ain't that something about easy-money DeYoung giving away his hogs?" Bruno said.

"He can write it all off," Art said. "As a loss. He'll make out in the end."

"You know what that means?" Bruno said.

"No."

"I don't either."

Art's cigarette was torn at the filter and he smoked it by

pinching the tear. He rested his arms on the shelf his stomach made.

"As a loss?" Bruno said. "How's he making out on shit if he don't sell the hogs. That's plainassed stupid."

Art waved Bruno away and handed him a sugar packet.

"Try this, you sour bastard," he said.

"Maybe you'll learn to stop telling jokes about Polacks needing to piss and looking for corners in round rooms."

They smiled and watched Miller and O'Brien reveal their lottery losses with pennies and curse the ticket and the governor himself. The black gum they'd scratched off flecked the table like an ant colony driven from its hill. Bruno counted thirty dollars worth of tickets and shook his head about money wasted. O'Brien pulled his cap brim over his eyes and swallowed tobacco juice. His hands were bigger than his feet.

"I don't know what the hell I'm doing here," O'Brien said. "All the winning tickets is up in Chicago. That's how they keep the niggers from burning the place down."

Miller spat on the floor and nodded.

"Yessir," he said. "A twenty-dollar winner keeps the niggers real peaceful. They really think they've won something."

"Shit," Bruno said, "the odds are right on the back of the ticket."

"Them's just figures," O'Brien said. "They don't mean nothing."

Bruno rolled his eyes and dropped two quarters on the counter and left the diner without a word. *They're both about as smart as Bob Lyon's boys.*

He walked the barditch home while the overcast moved down from the north as if a violent hooding of the earth. There were vague stars showing out east and they soon disappeared behind the unfolding clouds. An anemic light suffused the last clear horizon and soon the shadows died and the country was without silhouette until the moon rose and the barn lights and window lamps turned on the night.

Before he reached his lane across the blacktop he looked out over the fields in the dying light, the ground black and gored by plowblades. He knew that come summer the country flared a hundred shades of green and the crop leaves turned from the hot wind, but his memories of tiger lilies dotting the ditches and the potholes full from warm summer rains were like pictures he'd seen of a distant land. There was only the chill of this coming night and the woodsmoke that rose from the rooftops.

The dogs yelped high whines that told Bruno they'd not been fed. He cursed the boy and walked straight up the lane. The bare trees and curling woodvine made his house look inside of a cage. He stopped before a stranger sitting on the hackberry root jutting up from the mud. The man lifted his face from his hands. He was dirty like he'd been rained upon without ever drying. Luke's eyes were wet enough to shine where he stood in a puddle, looking at Bruno while the man rose.

"You come here for some wood?" Bruno asked.

"He didn't come here after any wood," Luke said.

"Mind your manners, boy," Bruno said. "Mind yourself."

The man stared at the flooded tire ruts. He was too slight in the shoulders to even be a man at all. Bruno thought of scarecrows left on abandoned farmsteads, crooked sticks knocked from trees. Luke watched them as if waiting for two cats to fight. The man finally looked at him: sad blue eyes, teeth dark as shale, his mouth bending a smile. Bruno stood there in the wind with his hat in his hand.

"Son of a bitch," he said.

Len came toward him and his arms were open to embrace. Bruno shoved his son back into the hackberry trunk, then ran off through the cut in the wire fence, heading toward the young oaks along Dog Creek. His heart bounced against his breast bone and he gestured to slow it by grabbing a handful of coat. For a moment he lost feeling in his arms and his throat tightened as if ice freezing in cisterns.

The field was flooded and the mooned overcast lay

mimed upon the water. Bruno went splashing through the swales until he stood knee deep and panted hard, halted long enough for the splash lines to vanish. The first small raindrops bothered the calm water. The wind was down. Len was making his way through the hedgerow, a small wrecked figure stumbling through the sinkholes while the last light diffused grimly in the narrowing gaps between the cloud formations. There seemed little about this boy turned man that justified Bruno's rage against him. He was river flotsam, the foamy scuz left to lap against the banked deadwood. The world had wrecked him in the way the rains stove down the green cornstalks. His body was only a remnant like the drowned corn offal whereupon the old man stood. He waited until Len was a small distance away and he could hear him breathe. The rain disappeared into their coats. Len pushed his coat sleeve up past his elbow and showed his arm in the darkness.

"I beat it," he said.

"You are a liar. You are still food for bigger things."

"I will make you see that I beat it."

"You are a ghost."

"I'm the one who's alive."

Len waded for him through the reflected clouds.

"I'll knock your ass down if you touch me again," Bruno said.

Luke was coming from the trees. He moved as if a shadow upon two legs, sluicing through the water while the clouds blew shut. The wind sucked in the oaks along the creek. The boy stopped short of them and jammed his hands deep into his field-jacket pockets.

"Go back, Luke," Bruno said. "This ain't nothing about you."

Len waded a half step closer.

"Bruce raped me," he said. "I bled and he laughed."

Bruno fetched back his hand and smacked Len with his open palm. Len offered his other cheek, crying while he smiled.

"Goddamn you," Bruno said.

He raised his hand again but the confused figure of Luke with quivering lips against the cold, flat way of the country bleared his eyes. The boy's face filled with horror, though not surprise, then he ran away, stepping hard as horses and whispering harshly to himself. He was imagining the rape, Bruno knew it, perhaps even feeling the blood leaking from him. The dark hedgerow swallowed him whole. The moonlight was coagulate in the cloud seams.

Len put his eyes into the old man's like stones being set together. Len took his hand, but his father pulled it back, his arm feeling numb as a stick.

"What do you want?" Bruno asked. "There ain't one thing a soul could want out here."

"Why won't you say what he did to me?" Len said.

The rain picked up and made loud sounds in the field water.

"Let him die," Bruno said.

"That isn't good enough," Len said.

The old man lit a cigarette and the orange from the guttering match wrapped around his cupped hand and through the glow he glimpsed his son's beard dripping in the darkness. He hated seeing him as a man and not a crooked fence post, a skinny dead tree.

Luke stood alone at the field's edge. There was hard wind now and sticks fell. The hickory branches, joined like folded hands, slowed the rain driving against his head. He looked up from his dark face in the darker water when Len walked toward the old man and embraced him. His grandfather held his arms straight as if he were a limbless tree. Len buried his face in the old man's muddy mackinaw and Luke waited for him to return the embrace, but he never did. He kicked the mud from his boots against a young hickory and walked to his car and got inside and drove away.

He headed north for Watega Town and drove a good distance up Grand Army of the Republic Highway before seeing that his headlights were off. He turned them on and the rain reeled in the long, widening beam. The starlight illuminated swaths of the flooded ditch where all kinds of flotsam bobbed upon the wavelets like refuse from a sunken ship. His eyes were unstrung and reflected that way in the windshield and he studied them while he drove. *Maybe he did what you said he did, you son of a bitch, but you got a father to teach you how to go the rest of the way. I got nothing now but your bloody asshole and the way my old man drew his eyes like a guttering fire when he got mean and wanted the whole world to feel like him. But you found your father and he never raped his brother for you to grow old knowing all about.*

The trailer stoop was made of loose cinderblocks and they separated while Luke stood knocking at the door. Pale light shone from the windows of the trailers across the gravel street. The fields were forever beyond. Luke was looking at his car when the door opened and Adonis Hill eyed him like movie drill sergeant.

"The way you knocked I thought you was a faggot looking for love," he said. "Knock again."

"Damn."

Adonis closed the door and Luke pounded on it with his fist.

"You got the balls you were born with now?" Adonis said.

"Goddammit, Hill."

Adonis sang from behind the aluminum door.

"Big balls, yah-hee, big balls. Talking to me, I got some big balls bigger than a tree. My big balls, they almost bigger than me."

"You gone dipshit?" Luke said.

Adonis was laughing and tying his tennis shoes when he opened the door. The television light made shifting shadows against the curtains where his stepfather sat half toothless on a green couch propped up by telephone books and catalogues. He drank vodka from a coffee cup and the plastic bottle was on the table next to him. The room was hazed with cigarette smoke. Adonis turned and saluted him. His stepfather only sat open-kneed with his hand around his throat like he choked himself and stared at the television.

Both his eyes closed. Adonis took his nylon coat off a framing nail pounded slantwise into the wall and closed the door.

"Aren't you going to tell him you're leaving?" Luke asked.

"Is it after six o'clock?" Adonis said.

"That was the Chicago news on TV."

"He's already forgot I live here."

"Shit, Hill."

"Go in and ask him," Adonis said. "Pretty soon he'll have on Channel 44 and start bitching about *The Honeymooners* being another rerun."

"They ain't made a new show of that since before we was born."

"Go in and ask him my name."

"I can't believe he wouldn't know your name," Luke said.

"What happened when I tried talking to him?"

"Both his eyes started closing."

"There you go, Konick," Adonis said.

They leaned against the car trunk in the cold wind. The rain quit but the dark air they breathed was wet, almost a vapor. Adonis patted his pockets for a cigarette. His coat was too big for his shoulders. Luke pointed back inside the trailer.

"What happened to him?" he said.

"The same thing that happened to your old man," Adonis said. "There wasn't much to start with. Then after a few letdowns, the rest is pretty much history."

"What's history?"

"Fucking hell, Konick," Adonis said. "Would you give me a cigarette?"

"He ever hit you?"

"I'm the one that hits him," Adonis said.

"He's never got drunk and hit you?"

"You might want to go over to the high school and see those people about a job. I bet you could skip right past college and start asking stoners a bunch of questions about their parents. Now give me a cigarette. The drunk's stole mine."

Luke smiled and tapped a Camel out of his soft pack.

They lit cigarettes while the cold starlight illuminated the gravel road that ran through the trailer park.

"What the hell happened to you last night?" Luke asked.

"That's my question to ask," Adonis said.

"They locked me up till morning after this big fat son of a bitch slapped me."

"How hard?"

"I felt like I was floating right there on the bench they set you on," Luke said.

In the sky the clouds opened and closed before the moon, and they watched as if they saw the winds way up high.

"Shit," Adonis said. "I just hid in the graveyard and waited for them bastards to leave. They looked for me a while, but not really that long."

"I didn't figure they would," Luke said.

The boys took the last draws off their cigarettes and flipped the butts against Adonis Hill's trailer and the glowing embers hissed cold against the corrugated aluminum. All the trailer windows held the same shifting television light.

"It sure gets dark around here," Luke said.

"People like it that way," Adonis said. "They live out here so everybody will forget them. It ain't the other way around like the teachers said."

"Nothing's like what the teachers said."

"Who told you it was supposed to be?"

"Nobody did, Hill. But I'm tired of finding out anyway."

They studied the flatness of the country about them and breathed cold while the stars appeared and disappeared behind slag clouds.

"You ever think one day it'll just be dark?" Luke asked.

"When you wake up dead," Adonis said.

"You think you'll know that you're dead?"

"I hope the fuck not."

"You don't believe in Heaven or none of that?"

"It ain't like a new town. If that's what you think."

"What is it, then?" Luke said.

"You make my head hurt."

Luke laughed and opened the trunk without telling
Adonis to move and it cuffed him in the backside. From
beneath the spare tire he took out the wrist-rocket and the
leather bag of ball bearings. Adonis Hill stopped cussing and
gave a little smile but Luke stowed it in his field jacket.

"Sounds like a gunshot when it hits anything," Luke said.

"No way."

"Just like a gunshot. You ready to do something to
LaFrance?"

"Fuck me, Konick. I never thought you were the type."

"He usually sits up on Grant Street at night waiting for
the drunks to drive home from the bars," Luke said. "We
could lay up by the railroad tracks and send two into his tail-
lights and hope he draws his gun."

"You've gone crazy."

"We could stalk the son of a bitch nightly."

"Then what?" Adonis said. "Blow up the high school?"

"We're joining the Marine Corps then."

"I never said nothing about the marines."

"You'd rather drive around drinking whatever a wino will
buy for you?"

"I can buy whatever I want after I'm twenty-one."

"And sit in all these bars, too. Maybe we could join one of
those pool teams and bet our paychecks from the lumber-
yard."

Adonis stared at the ground.

"You at least interested in getting that cop?" Luke asked.

Adonis spat in the weeds snarling up from the gravel
street and looked up, cawing like a crow.

The moon was swirled by clouds while they drove into
town with their reflections smeared boy beside boy across
the windshield. Luke parked on Forest Avenue where the
glass block windows from empty warehouses turned the
rain, and they walked the alley out to the railroad trestle
that crossed Grant Street and the dark, mottled water of the

Watega River. The night warmed and a yellow fog nuzzled the dripping bungalows. The alley ended against a weedy slope and they climbed it silently and used scrub oaks for handholds and the trees pulled taut and their roots gave in the mud.

Luke crested the slope first and gave Adonis a hand and pulled him the rest of the way. He felt his friend's pulse surge through his palm even after he'd let go. Adonis stood straight on the tracks and gave the stars back their bleak and distant stare. Luke surveyed the river to the west, walled by hardwoods and brownbrier, then the squat bungalows back east where silhouettes of people slid across the yellow windowpanes. He took the wrist-rocket from his field jacket and Adonis watched him with wide eyes.

"Can you hit anything with it?" Adonis said.

"A car's pretty big to miss," Luke said. "It'll be sitting still."

"And that bucketheaded son of a bitch jacking himself off."

"I don't think LaFrance is the type," Luke said. "He's the judge of right and wrong."

"He's the judge of my asshole."

Luke heard rain in the wind and the cars down on Grant Street. Beyond the rooftops were the smokestacks from General Foods with their endless columns of steam that twisted and righted in the wind. Adonis blew a plume of cold and looked around.

"We sure are high up here," Luke said.

"It's easy to be high when everything is flat," Adonis said. "That's the law of differences."

"My ass."

"It sounded right to say," Adonis said.

"I know when I'm up high and it ain't got nothing to do with how flat everything is," Luke said.

They sat in the scrub trees so they could see the roadside where LaFrance parked to pick off drunks. Adonis threw gravel at the hoary weeds and they heard rabbits run down the slope but saw nothing of them. Luke loaded the wrist-rocket with a ball bearing and held it across his lap, ready to shoot. Adonis patted his pockets for a cigarette as was his habit when he didn't have any to smoke.

"Give me a cigarette, Konick," he said.

"It ain't tactical."

"What the hell?"

"In the movies whenever some guy smokes at night a German sniper shoots him deader than shit."

"That's when somebody is looking for you and nobody gives a shit about us. You're just too lazy to move your hands."

"Go on," Luke said. "They're in my top pocket."

Adonis smoked and sat against the tree with his knees up. Luke lay on his side before a log and watched the street. Cars were coming out of the fog and speeding away around the curb.

"What made you all happy about doing this?" Adonis asked. "I always thought you just took things."

"When did you see me just take it?" Luke said.

"The time Steve Brown caught you looking at his girl-friend's tits and slapped you in front of the whole cafeteria. You stood there and looked at him with his hand mark on your cheek."

The night birds cawed from the trees across the street. Adonis raised his ears to the sound like a dog. Luke sat up against the log and pulled the wrist-rocket taut.

"You ever think real hard about living?" he said.

"Not like you."

"I mean, how some people always get kicked around and others do the kicking. There's also people who sit and smile and nothing ever happens to them."

"Something happens to everybody, Konick."

"Not that cop," Luke said. "I bet he never went to Vietnam."

"I wouldn't have, either," Adonis said. "I ain't fighting in no army. Next war, I'm going way up to the Yukon and get-ting me a cabin and a dog."

"They'd just find you and turn you back."

"I saw a map and there ain't no place to start looking," Adonis said.

"Probably."

"Probably, shit," Adonis said. "There ain't no roads for cops to drive down after you. What cop you know would climb mountains to arrest anybody?"

"They got some good cops up there," Luke said.

"A cop is the same everywhere."

The wind dropped down from the treetops and laid flat the gray weeds. Luke rolled to his elbows and lay in the mud listening.

"So you think I ain't doing this for anybody?" he said.

"I don't know," Adonis said. "Some people like beatings so they got a reason to drink and stare at the TV set. I think you're up here playing soldier more than anything else."

"There ain't nothing wrong with being a soldier," Luke said. "I'd go if I was called."

"That's stupid, Konick. Anybody can go when they're called. What's special about that?"

Grant Street was quiet for an hour while Luke lay anxiously in the mud and Adonis slept with slow breath and the rain trickled down his cheeks. He was just a shape lying there, nothing more than the scrub trees that twisted about them. Luke's skin bumped and his eyes ran. He came to his knees but was only colder and shook so badly that he saw his hands move. Within five minutes, twelve cars passed that resembled police cruisers, rearing from the fog with square chassis and windshields shining dashlight. Then LaFrance came around the curb where the river broke white over limestone rocks, and he stopped in the right lane. His brakelights made red puddles on the street. Luke went prone behind the log and raised his head slowly, then kicked Adonis in his heel. When he came awake, Luke had a finger over his lips.

"What's he doing just sitting there in the street?" Adonis said.

Luke motioned with his hand for him to lay flat. LaFrance reversed on the grass and his headlights bounced against the trees while he rolled over the curb. The clouds closed in the sky and the shadow of the trestle was gone with the moon-wash on the street. LaFrance was dusky behind the window and the radio lights tinted his face green. Luke came to his knees with the wrist-rocket and aimed for the right taillight when some dogs started up. Adonis grabbed his arm.

"You know what these cops will do to us?" he said.

Luke looked back at the lamplit houses. He pulled the rubber back past his shoulder.

"We're getting out of here the same way we came in," he said.

"Wait up, Konick."

"Just follow me out of here."

Adonis grabbed Luke's shoulder, but he pushed back and knocked him sideways in the mud. Dogs were beginning to bark all through the neighborhood. He got up and breathed wildly and tried throwing himself on Luke but Luke leaned low and Adonis sprawled flat on their footprints, his shirt-tail untucked and showing pale skin. He grabbed for Luke's ankle but Luke kicked his hand.

"Get off me," Luke said.

"You son of a bitch," Adonis said. "You crazy son of a bitch."

Luke let the shot go and the rubber snapped forward with quiet violence and the taillight popped. He reloaded quickly, losing a ball bearing from his palm. The second shot rico-cheted off the bumper. LaFrance was looking around the cruiser when Luke shattered the back window.

"Shit," Adonis said.

Luke drew down on LaFrance while he stepped from the cruiser and slipped in the mud. His maglight went rolling off into the curb and turned the gutter water white. He scurried to cover himself behind the open door, but slipped again, landing face down in a weedy puddle. His pistol belt was twisted about his waist so that his nightstick stuck out between his thighs. Cars slowed past him, honking their horns, but none stopped. The radio dispatcher begged him to respond. He came to his knees with the pistol drawn and the mud slimed his uniform. Luke felt alive, like he was getting a girl naked, and all the nerves and the fear of saying something wrong had vanished. Now, it was all strangely natural. *I am Luke Konick, you pig motherfucker* He had LaFrance and imagined the ball bearing goring his fat cheeks, but before he released the shot, Adonis knocked away his arm and it was lost. A pistol report sounded and mud jumped near the log.

They were running down the tracks in file when the first siren sound. Their footfalls splashed the puddles between the ties. Soldier's Creek rose halfway up the trestle piers and the sirens quit when they crossed it. The board used for a footbridge had floated away. Luke felt alive and sprinted through the fog, then slowed for Adonis to catch him. Adonis ran open-mouthed and gasped at the wet air to fill his lungs. He held his stomach and leaned sideways, coughing while he breathed.

"You motherfucker," Adonis said.

"Get down," Luke said.

"You was going to kill that cop."

Luke grabbed Adonis by the forearm and pulled him off the tracks into the weeds. The street began thirty feet away and all of the trees dripped rain and suddenly the blue police lights were spinning against the fog. The alleys from the neighborhood behind them ran up to the railroad tracks and there were more blue lights strafing the wet garages. Luke heard the rain tapping the cruiser hoods and smelled the lingering exhaust and, when he listened closely, the squelch breaking on the radios. He could not see down the creek because the fog hung close to the dark water and he knew the banks were flooded. Adonis tried talking but he gagged and retched clear bile in the mud.

"They ain't on foot," Luke said. "The blue lights are still moving."

Adonis lifted his face to see. He spat. Mud and vomit dripped from his chin.

"I can't even believe you," he said.

Luke was sure they could have gotten away through the alleys if Adonis had run faster, but now they were cut off. He should have done this alone. The cops on Grant Street were working their strobe lights against the tracks; the poled beams crossed and recrossed in the fog. The only way out was down the creek where the darkness hung total and they could follow it out of town into the Perry Woods.

"Them cops will beat us stupid," Adonis said.

"Probably. If they get us."

"I thought all you was going to do was shoot once and run," Adonis said.

The two of them lay in the weeds breathing up the darkness. The mud smelled rotten from the long weeks of rain.

"We better get into the creek," Luke said.

"Shit, no."

"Just hold on to my belt and move as slow as I do."

Adonis did not move. He was visibly frightened by Luke.

"You see a better way out?" Luke said.

"You wanted to kill him. I saw it."

"I ain't ashamed of myself."

"The bullet kicked mud on my leg," Adonis said.

"Keep hold of my belt," Luke said.

They slithered on their bellies down the slope before slipping into the water, boy behind boy, the way snakes slide off rocks. The cops were walking the tracks with maglights and working them down into the creek, but Luke knew the fog was thick and yellow and would hold the shine above them the way a sponge did water. The wind drove the rain and everywhere was the taste of the strange flotsam.

Dawn was not far away when they came from the woods and dark sky sank about the fields and they followed a creek that wound through the country but seemed a straight line while they walked it. The wind turned cold

and it was raining. They'd spent the night without a fire
and buried themselves in brown pine needles and lay back
against back while the rain bore into them as if they were
deadfall and the wind sounded different in the odd-sized
trees. Their jeans were stiff with mud and nests of leaves
stuck to their shoes. Adonis walked small and erect with
his hands pulled up into his coat sleeves because he had
no gloves. Luke swung a stick too thin for use as a weapon
or a cane. All night he told Adonis that feeling the cold
meant only that they were very alive. Adonis had said
nothing and hugged his knees and shook violently.

The bungalows and the filthy woodframes appeared
upon the flat plain. The creek went underground into a corrugated drainage pipe. They left the fields and walked the
alleys of crushed gravel and passed garages spray-painted
with hysterical graffiti. Adonis lagged behind in the darkness and Luke did not see him when he spoke. His words
were accented by chattering teeth.

"You sure the marines send you to California?" he asked.

"San Diego," Luke said.

"Did the guy tell you that to your face?"

"He ain't your dope-smoking buddy," Luke said. "He's a
gunnery sergeant. That's what you call him."

"He could be a retarded midget and I wouldn't care if he
sent me to California."

"I wouldn't tell him that."

"Shit, Konick. I could call his momma a hairy, ape-faced
bitch and he'd smile and enlist me. He's nothing but a sales-
man and if he don't sell I bet his boss rides his ass."

"He ain't unloading cars."

"No. He's selling being in the marines."

The morning paled above the rooftops while they took
the alleys straight into town. The recruiting office was
closed when they got there. They waited in a dark doorway
and all the streetlights along Court Street glowed vaguely
while milk trucks and bakery vans sped across the river to
the diners by the factories. They lit cigarettes and smoked

them cupped in their hands when the hallway light illuminated and the recruiting sergeant stood looking at them through the glass door. The creases in his khaki shirt sliced midway through his pockets and were sharp from heavy starch. The toes of his low-quarter shoes glinted and held color like his belt buckle. He turned the lock and opened the door.

"Even a dumbass boot knows to come in from the rain," he said.

Luke dropped his cigarette and smiled shyly. Adonis went on smoking.

"But being you already like the mud," the sergeant said, "I'll call the commandant myself and tell him we got two for the infantry. But you boys could be fancy fuckers in disguise. If that's affirmative I better keep my back against the wall and tell you to wait for the air force recruiter. Them baby blue uniforms are sure pretty."

Luke looked at the sergeant and felt his own doe eyes and tried hardening them. *I bet you don't feel nothing you don't want to feel. I bet they taught you how to order it right out of your head.*

"Sir, my name's Luke Konick," he said. "I told you I'd come back with my buddy."

The sergeant studied him with his cold blue eyes.

"I remember you, double-dog," he said. "You were the one who wanted a sword."

"Yessir."

The sergeant looked at Adonis while Adonis drew his cigarette and hacked wet from his lungs.

"You eighteen?" the sergeant asked.

"I'm almost nineteen," Adonis said. "And I ain't signing nothing unless I know for sure I'm going to California."

"You'll start out at Marine Corps Recruit Depot in San Diego, California."

"Do I get to stay?" Adonis said.

"You just tell your drill instructor how much you love MCRD and he'll put your name on the A-list."

"How will I know which one's him?"

Luke watched the sergeant trying not to laugh at Adonis and his muddy tennis shoes held together by electrical tape.

"Your drill instructor will introduce himself the very first day," the sergeant said.

"Will he be around the rest of the time?" Adonis said. "I want get on that list ahead of all the brown-nosers."

"You won't get shut of him," the sergeant replied. "He'll be like your mother."

"Shit," Adonis said. "She ran off."

"They'll throw him in naval prison if he does."

Adonis grinned like he found the angle.

"When can we go?" Luke said.

"I can drive you to Chicago myself to test and take your physical soon as you come back here cleaned up," the sergeant said.

"We can't go home," Luke said.

"I bet you don't got a dollar between you," the sergeant said.

They both shook their heads.

"You boys got police records?"

"I've been arrested," Luke said.

"They take your prints or charge you with anything?"

"No."

"You're clean."

The sergeant took out his wallet and handed Luke a twenty-dollar bill.

"You take your little buddy to the Salvation Army next door when it opens and see what clothes you can find," he said. "There's a shower in the head."

"A head?" Adonis said.

"It's what you better start calling the can," the sergeant said.

"I can pay you back the money," Luke said.

"We'll talk about that in my office. We got a shitload of papers to start drawing up."

The old man stood in the toolshed and held a match to the lantern wick but did not light it. The flame spindled down the stick and he dropped it when his fingertip blistered. He faintly smelled his burned flesh but he never looked away from the window. There was a mist after the rains quit and across the open country the mist was white from the moon and as cold. The Whizzer frame hung from the ceiling by bent coat hangers, ready to paint, but he did not look at it. He dreamed of his birches and the falling snow and the way as a boy he wandered the woods lost in the white and thinking himself not a body at all, but a color, untouchable by even the wind. Back then nothing from this world stuck to him.

His son was in the house after thirteen years and he wished he could think of his birches more than that. He broke out in the field and let Len come inside where they faced each other in thigh-deep water. His son stared at him with eyes so afraid, not knowing where to look. But that wasn't what did it; the old man still had the pose of a boxer, warning Len not to hug him again. It was what his son asked that made him lower his fists. Len wiped his swollen eyes, the mud, tears, and rain jelled upon his cheeks, then said: "Can I watch you sand away the rust from those old tools and listen to you tell me what the tool was used for and why men don't need them anymore? I'll go then. I won't come back." The old man put a finger to his lips and watched the scarves of fog drift past his house. "Come on," he said to Len. "It's a fool thing to stand out here ass deep in this water."

The old man lit a cigarette and watched the match burn itself cold on the toolshed floor. He made arcs with the cigarette ember, arcs within arcs. He looked out the window for deer to come through the fog even though he knew there was one more week of the hunting season and the deer would hide in places only they knew. He wondered if the does and the bucks felt like a war was over when they saw no more men in day-glo vests waiting for them in tree stands. He knew the war in Europe was over when he heard bird songs in the woods, by the wind turning the green beech leaves, the grass smells, the gray squirrels running along tree limbs, the confused flight of sparrows in the warm countryside. There was nothing else about the country to convince him that the killing was over. In the cowless pastures remained the muddy imprints of the German wounded where they lay the last hours of the war waiting to die. The roads were ruined by the retreating Panzer columns. The spring grass was marred by a thousand bootprints.

That day he was neither a sergeant of infantry nor a white-tailed deer. He was simply Bruno Konick from Watega, Illinois, out walking to walk so he could look at the trees and breathe the sunlit air. There was rain in the night and the apple trees bloomed by the roadside. He looked at the trees and the forest floor still laden with mines and called the trees by name and their names he remembered slowly as if recalling a forgotten language.

He left the road when he heard water running over rocks,

drunk on the smell of apple blossoms and thinking nothing of land mines. The orchard was untended. The beech trees in the small forest beyond were marred by grenade shrapnel; rifle bullets had flecked the bark. He found the creek and upstream the water went from green to white over the jagged rocks. Shell casings were strewn upon the forest floor like acorns, and in the tree shadows were the cast-off helmets from two armies, not yet rusted. He knelt and touched the cool water and splashed it with his hand and studied his reflected face while the water calmed. He looked about the forest and nothing looked back.

He undid his web belt and took the .45 from its holster and laid the belt on the grass and then set down the pistol. He took off his boots and rolled his pant legs and took up the .45 and waded thin, tired, and dreamy into the creek. His feet were very white in the greenish water where the minnows scattered. He then stripped down to his GI skivvies and the sun and wind were gentle on his white skin. He waded out for the deep water so he could immerse himself and watch the last four years rise off him like mud from a rock, then sat down. The water was cold from the spring rains and it moved quickly about him, foamy where it passed around deadfall. He cupped his hands and drank from the creek while the filth rose from his shorts. He lay the pistol on a log and took a breath before going backward into the water. He kept his eyes open. The minnows slid over his shins, his cheeks, and a small turtle swam over his chest.

He came from the water when he could no longer hold his breath. Two men stood on the bank, shadowed by the budding trees, while birds flew into the orchard. They wore the striped pants of the camps and hard jack boots and the black tunics of the SS. Potato-masher grenades were slung through their rope belts. They held Lugers. He rose dripping from the creek and smiled. They looked like twins—shaved heads, lips wrecked by chancres, pale skin stretched over the contours of their skulls. He waded toward the bank with the .45 ready in his hand.

"Speak English?" he said.

One of them said that he did. His friend was a young boy who smiled shyly to hide his rotten teeth.

"Good," Bruno said. "Because I can't understand none of your talk."

"Neither can he," said the man of the boy. "We speak in the German of the camps. Fifty words is all we have between us."

The boy pointed at his U.S. Army uniform hanging on a bush and smiled so wide his eyes half closed. He handed Bruno his clothes and Bruno nodded his thanks. The boy had no eyelashes. His fingernails were missing. The man wore the Star of David stitched crudely over the Nazi eagle on the black tunic. There was a crook to his jaw, and his chin was missing as if it had been chipped away.

Bruno dressed and stepped sockless into his boots and when he was done, the man nodded.

"Do not take off your boots for a long time here," the man said. His accent was French, his lips black with scabs.

"The whole shitting thing is over," Bruno said. "Everybody can go ahead and take off their boots. We got all these Kraut soldiers clearing the minefields. Before long you won't even know there was a war here."

The boy stared open-mouthed at Bruno as if he saw a movie star. The man shook his head and stepped from the tree shadows into the sunlight. The boy tried closing his mouth but he could not.

"There are still men in these woods who will kill you," the man said. "I shot one by this creek last night. He was a Dane and I saw him sitting on a log trying to burn the SS tattoo off his bicep with a hot bayonet. I walked right up to him and shot him in the face and then kicked him into the fire. I am sure he would have returned to Denmark and lived his life telling all who asked he only drove a truck in Berlin."

Bruno had watched the man's face contort while he told the story. They boy was anxious, perhaps trying to remember the few English words he knew to ask a question.

"We ain't seen no stray SS on our patrols," Bruno said. "They've been surrendering real regular. They come to us on their own, real thankful the Russians or the French didn't get them first."

"Are you calling me a liar?" the man asked.

"To look at you tells me the truth," Bruno said.

"There are many SS who are not German. They are afraid to go home. Many Swedes. Many French. I have heard Berlin was defended until the last by men like these."

"If you get caught killing an ex-SS," Bruno said, "they'll try you for regular murder."

"You are ex-SS like you can be an ex-man."

"It's all over. We got roomfuls of German officers sitting around looking worried. They'll do anything for a cigarette. Some will even pose for pictures in the full Nazi salute."

"You are like your movies, Joe," the man said. "What cowboy can ride away after what happened here?"

Bruno moved the pistol between his hands to put on his shirt. After he dressed, he sat down on a log and the boy and the man sat in the grass and he passed around cigarettes which they all lit off the same match.

"You boys going home?" he asked.

"In time I will," the man said. "But the boy is a Jew from Poland."

"He can go home if he wants."

"The Poles will kill him. The Jews of Paris and Brussels think that he is a donkey, a stupid Yid. Our war has only started."

The boy smiled like they were telling jokes.

"You two can't do nothing alone," Bruno said.

"There are many of us in the woods," the man said. "You will hang the generals when it is the corporals we seek."

"How you going to know who's the right corporal?"

"The way they knew who was the right Jew."

The man shrugged his shoulders. The boy smoked and grinned and perhaps thought the conversation was about something else.

"We got orders to take your guns," Bruno said. "Higher is going out of its way not to piss off the German people."

"Take our guns?" the man said. "Will they also make us men again?"

"I didn't say I was going to. I don't really care. After I get home, the whole thing will be like a dream I forget by lunchtime."

"Then you, Joe," the man said, "have never really dreamed before. But you will. One day you will wonder if the world of sleep is not more real than being awake."

"I don't know what you're talking about," Bruno said.

"You will be walking along and suddenly you are in a different place than where you think you might be. You will have such nightmares at noon."

"Shit," Bruno said. "That's crazy."

The boy looked at the sun where he sat on the grass beneath some thick beech trees. He was song-eyed, as if drunk on the smell of apple blossoms. He began speaking in German, the words coming slowly, and he smiled to show his missing bottom teeth. Bruno also smelled the apple blossoms and the last of the night rain upon the petals and he wondered what about these scents made the boy so happy. The man nodded and watched their cigarette smoke vanish into sunlight, then looked at Bruno. They all held their pistols.

"He wants to know what it is like to kill an SS," the man said. "He has not yet shot one. He wonders if it is not like having a girl—an American girl with beautiful teeth. I cannot answer his question because I have not had such a girl."

The boy looked eagerly at Bruno.

"Not all of them have pretty teeth," Bruno said.

"The boy came to Buchenwald from Auschwitz in the winter," the man said. "He had no shoes. Please, tell him it is so."

"Auschwitz?" Bruno said.

"It is in Poland," the man said. "Now tell him it is so."

Bruno looked at the boy's rotten teeth and nodded that it was true. The boy lay back on the grass. He looked angelic in the hard morning light.

"Can I ask you something?" Bruno said to the man.

"Yes."

They both watched the boy aim his pistol at sparrows on the beech limbs.

"Did you leave that dead man in the creek?" Bruno asked.

"In the creek where you were bathing."

"I thought you said you left him in the fire."

"I waited until his face was burned away, then I kicked him in the water and watched him steam."

The weather turned overnight and come morning the sky was bluer than lake water. Len stood by the woodpile with the sun in his eyes as if to cleanse the way he saw this house. The ax felt both strange and familiar in his hands and its smooth handle rubbed a blister on his palm. The logs he'd split lay strewn in the wet grass. He leaned the ax against a cord of ash and pulled away the bark from a log and stared at six white, membranous grubs. They were alive and he shook it to knock them into the grass but the grubs would not fall away. He cocked his arm to send the log spinning into the field mud but brought it back down and touched each grub before setting the log back on the pile.

Len was watching the wind sweep the dead weeds along the fence when his father came walking fast from the cherry trees. The old man was dressed no better than a scarecrow.

He clenched a cold pipe between his teeth. His palms were scaled with calluses. Without words, the old man quickly stacked the logs two at a time into a perfect cord and then filled the pipe from a plastic baggy. Len counted the years since they last met eyes in daylight. The old man drew smoke and one wisp stirred under the cap brim.

"You was always a good worker until something caught your eyes," he said. "I always thought to put horse blinders on you."

Len forced a smile when he understood how lean and bitter the old man had become. He saw it in small things. The way his pipe bounced from his lips. How he never looked at anything directly out of disappointment over what he kept seeing.

"I'd tell you to glance up and keep working," the old man said. "But you always stopped and looked full at it. You remember when we was roofing barns with Art Bertrand and you kept talking about how pretty it was the way the sunlight fell on the cornstalks? Shit. Art just looked at you and said that the sunlight fell yesterday and it will fall again tomorrow but the job's got to be done today. You about cried. The boy's like that."

"You heard from him?" Len said.

The old man turned suddenly as if hearing an accident down on the road. He took the pipe from his mouth and tapped the bowl with a twig he kept in his pocket.

"I can't enjoy nothing when there's work to be done," he said. "When I was building barns after the war, there was men who could sleep through lunch. I never understood that."

"You think Luke will come back?" Len said.

The old man nodded and relit his pipe.

"About a month ago," he said, "there were still green weeds and the trees were full of leaves. Then it got cold as January and these two big snows come. The farmers wrote off everything. But the deer made out for a few days. They were about the only ones. At night I'd see big herds coming into the fields after the corn. Sometimes there was twenty of them at a time crossing the road like school kids. You'd see deer that were crazy looking; some had antlers sticking out the middle of their heads. Inbreeding, I'd guess. The herds have gotten too big since you can't hunt them but two weekends a year. Then they started getting hit by trucks. But Art Bertrand said he saw a timber wolf a few nights ago. I asked him if he was sure it wasn't no dog and he swears it came up over his waist. Now a couple wolves would thin the deer out."

"We can do better than this," Len said.

The old man shook the dead embers in his pipe bowl.

"I could tell you I'm sorry," he said. "But if I was you I'd whip my ass for saying something that ignorant. Anyway, it's time for my walk. You can either come with me or stay here looking off at the trees."

"What about Luke?"

"I guess he'll be back since he don't got a five-dollar bill in his pocket. He can let himself in the house."

They stood against the woodpile and looked past each other like strangers at a bar. The old man took off walking without a word and Len followed him down the length of brown grass that separated two farmers' cornfields. The river trees illuminated yellow and faded quietly with the clouds passing before the sun and the branches trembled in the wind and made sounds like the speech of ghosts. Soon the clouds cleared and they crossed a broad pasture of windswept grass hemmed by a vacant blue sky. Their boot-falls made no sounds in the grass and the sky itself was like a sea above them and Len daydreamed they wandered the floor of a great ocean.

The old man loosened his scowl when they came to a ruined farmstead. The wind laid flat the gray weeds over the limestone footings left from the house and the barn. Len saw the faint traces of the lane heading off toward Leggtown Road. Two deer sunned themselves, dappled by willow shadows, but the thick-necked bucks broke for the cover in the river trees when the wind gusted violently and spread their human scent. The old man grabbed Len by the coat sleeve and pointed out the two deer, now only moving blurs. Len listened while his father counted their points aloud and noted their white markings. With the wind came dark clouds that rose in the north as if a mountain range forever beyond daylight. The old man pointed at the limestone with a crooked finger and etched upon the air where the house and the barn had once supported life.

"Do you know where you are?" he asked.

Len wiped the wind blear from his left eye. "This was your grandpa's farm," he said.

"He never owned it a day."

"But he worked it as a tenant farmer."

"That don't mean shit," the old man said. "A tenant farmer is what you call a white sharecropper. Back then you had to make them distinctions."

Len turned away from the wind while it shifted as if chasing him. The old man wiped the pipe stem off on his blue jeans and pointed with it.

"My dad died two Sundays after Easter on them footings," he said. "There was snow and lightning together that day. I watched it over them willow trees where the deer were."

The old man coughed from breathing weed chaff in the air. He spoke about tornadoes that left ten-acre swaths through the green fields and told of droughts when the ground cracked and many believed the winds were eroding the earth and the world might crumble like dry leaves. When the locusts came in the summer of 1933, the wall-eyed revival minister from Kansas convinced thirty Catholic farmers in a tent one night that the end was upon them. They were born again after he baptized them in the Watega River and many went stone deaf from ear infections because the water was stagnant from the drought. The priests refused to visit them and even forgot their names until the World War I veterans got their bonus checks and sanctuaries needed new rugs. The old man pointed out where the

142

first barn stood before it burned one dry winter day and he showed how he and his grandfather had driven the livestock down to the creek and the way they drug his father back to the house after he'd collapsed in the barn with a cigarette, dazed from coughing.

"My father was from someplace in Poland," the old man said. "I was never sure where. He knew less than a hundred words of English on the day he died. He was in France during the first war and they made him a bicycle messenger because the army figured he didn't need to know English to deliver slips of paper. I know he got gassed on the Muese and come back in 1919 too sick to work. He spit blood the way men spit tobacco juice. I was a boy when he died."

"What happened to your mother?" Len said.

"She was too quiet to leave me with any memories. One of them women who lived her life without volume and never untied her apron. She was more my father's nurse than his wife. She died when I was in North Africa, living in a rooming house and talking to her socks. The landlady told me she was."

Two crows landed on the footings. The old man closed his eyes and opened them. His left hand trembled and he stayed it with his right hand and then helped it into his pants pocket. Len looked at him and looked at the crows.

"I don't understand why you came back here after the war," Len said.

"For a time I thought I fought for Watega County and it was just God-given that I come back. We figured we had certain claims to things because we'd been overseas, but so did everybody else. Some came back to settle scores that were four years old on account of the war and there were some fistfights that fall of 1945. They were mostly over women who quit them for the 4-Fs. There were some murders. The boys who'd been in the Pacific were real squirrelly.

"Coming home we were packed into train cars out of Fort Dix and New York City worse than we were in troop ships going over in 1942. We smoked Camels and passed whiskey pints and there were big card games on the back of uniform jackets—hundred-dollar pots and nobody gave a shit if they were losing. Everybody was laughing but not from being happy. None of it was a year old yet. We didn't really know what we'd saw or done. But the boys got real quiet the closer we came to Illinois. It was like someone turned off a light. We were all drunk but the laughing was over. Then these farmboys started getting off the train in Cleveland and Toledo with weird looks on their faces, like they couldn't see two feet away. They left quietly and faded off into the dark stations with barracks bags slung over their shoulders.

"There was only four of us left when we made Chicago— me and this kid from Charbonneau named Delwood Cleaver and two Italians from Joliet. Cleaver had his ear-lobe burned off somewhere along the Elbe and got so cry-ing drunk that he drooled and burned his pants full of cigarette holes. He wouldn't shut up about how they give the land that cost him an earlobe right back to the Russians. He got off the train at Union Station and that was the last I heard of him. I was glad. I couldn't take his crying no more. Neither could the Italians."

The old man went quiet and started walking. They fol-lowed the creek toward the river and stopped amid the water sounds and Len noticed his father's hands were more veiny than autumn leaves and they trembled again. The wind blew wide lines in the Watega River and the cold sun-light brightened the water beyond the tree shadows where it was deep. The old man took a stone from his pocket and stared off for a long second, then threw the stone off across the water, but it fell short because of the wind. Len buttoned his coat and watched his father hold his hands together to keep them from shaking.

"There was this hard rain the night you were born," the old man said. "You came in the dark after the storm set in real good. Your head was out before Doc Haig even got there and you stopped and waited for him. You didn't seem to want any part of what you were coming into. Your mother didn't even care. You would have thought she was birthing a rat the way she acted. I never did nothing but try to love her. Then Doc Haig pulled up in his 1940 Ford with them patched victory tires and he didn't have his yellow slicker off before he was unwinding you from the umbilical chord. Haig was about forty-five then, skinny with this oblong face that was always pissed off. He spent his doctoring life treating hayshakers that couldn't pay or cutting the legs off marines who tripped land mines in the Pacific. He drove that Ford until Ike was president.

"I tied Bruce to his crib with some lashing rope to keep him away from your mother. He was screaming and holding his breath until his face looked like a bruise. Your mom couldn't take hollering of any kind so I ran a sock around his mouth to quiet him. His lips were slick with blood from biting his own tongue. Doc Haig saw him that way, his hands wet from the rain and the blue slime that came off you. Bruce was bound like a little hostage and giving the rope hell. Haig said he was going to law me if I didn't untie him. I'd told him three times that he kept wanting to hug his mother while she was in labor. He looked at me in that smug-ass way of doctors and asked me why I didn't just close the door. Shit, I said. I tried it. The little asshole would have been out the window young as he was.

"The rain quit after Haig got your mother to finally nurse you. I'd untied Bruce and held him by his waist in the doorway. He bit and flailed his arms. I swear he didn't want her touching you. She had the look in her eye the way a hooker does when she says not to kiss her. She handed you off to Doc Haig as fast as she could and stared at her gray eyes reflected in the window glass until he gave her a shot.

"I paid Haig his ten dollars and he took it without looking at me. I went to shake his hand but he put on his slicker and left. He wanted out of there and I can't say I blamed him. We were something to see, even for a navy doctor who cleaned up after Okinawa. I'm sure he'd seen other couples like us.

We were together because we were the only ones left. But I stood on the porch after Doc Haig drove away, holding you when you weren't three hours old. It was dark and the clouds opened after the rain and there were stars like dreams and the moon was so full its light lay along the tree branches. For a while there was only you and me and the mist low upon the summer fields."

Len looked at his father after he went silent. The sadness remained with him like a lodger. The wind shook a dead tree rooted in the bankside water and the trunk was barkless and white as teeth. The old man beat his pipe against it and watched the migrant weeds blow across the Watega. Len waited for him to ask about his years in Chicago, but he never did.

"It's ignorant to stand out here with a storm blowing in," the old man said.

"The clouds are two hours off," Len said.

The old man walked away and Len followed him through a wasted pumpkin field to Leggtown Road and headed for Saint Marie. In town the streets were matted with hoary weeds and the neon beer signs in Hubert's windows left red light on the sidewalk. Mexicans looked at them from mangled pickups parked outside the late-run movie theater and waited on their fat wives in the laundromat. The blank marquees had face-sized holes where sparrows nested. Weeds lay along the wiper blades of the few cars parked against the curb.

Art Bertrand came from his diner when they crossed Grant Street. He sipped from a coffee mug. His black socks were rolled in tubes around his flaked ankles. He looked spooked, like a cat caught in the rain.

"You were going to walk past your old pal," he said. "I saw you."

"Maybe I was," the old man said. "Maybe I wasn't. But I must admit them anklets make you one good-looking son of a bitch."

"It like to have rained weeds this morning," Art said.

The old man nodded with a mean smile. Art studied Len like he knew him, but looked away shaking his head.

"No, Bruno," Art said. "I mean weeds was the air and the air was weeds. The sky got this weird red like something was going to come riding from it. You couldn't see them Mexicans across the street. I never saw anything close to it."

"We got a few things left to see," the old man said.

"You know the millennium is seventeen years off."

"Shit. You've been listening to that radio preacher again. Last winter he had you thinking God turned off the sun. Then come summer you think he's burning us out."

"With all the wars and hunger," Art said, "I think something's coming anytime."

"Weatherman calls it rain."

"You're an asshole, Bruno."

The old man waved Art away and left him in the diner doorway with his hands deeply pocketed. He was still standing there when they turned off Grant for the unswerving county road that went past the old man's lane. Weeds layered the water in the barditch. Len watched blackbirds coming into the fields from west of the road. He could hear more without seeing them, flocks of twenty.

"Art knew who I was," Len said.

His father gnawed his pipe. He kicked gravel into the barditch.

"He might of," he said.

"He's known me before I remember knowing him."

"Don't bank on him remembering. He couldn't find his ass with both hands."

"I'm your son," Len said.

"I ain't ready for his questions."

"You just aren't ready to say Bruce did it."

The old man's finger shook while he pointed at the wrecked fields.

"Look at what the rain and ice did to that man's crops," he said. "Look at them cornstalks all shredded and twisted and heaped in the mud like mangled men. Nature is a killer."

"I've dreamed it different."

"We ain't nothing but them cornstalks, so what's the worth of one man's dreaming?"

"What did this to you?" Len said.

"I got to feed my dogs."

"I want to know some things."

"I'm the innkeeper here, goddammit."

They saw the brown squad car idling in the lane before they saw the sheriff's deputy looking through the house windows. He stood waist deep in the untended bushes with his hand over his eyes. The dogs' hackles had volume and so did their barking. Tire ruts went off into the woods behind the toolshed and looped around by the wood piles where two birch cords were knocked over. The tracks also fishtailed around the house and mud dripped off the clapboards. A young tree was crushed, half buried by the turned earth.

The old man seethed like a river in the rain. He walked to the house, showing teeth. The deputy was a high-waisted man with legs starting below his chest. He looked from the window and his brown pants were soaked from the wet bushes.

"What reason is there to have my grass all over your tires, Billadeau?" the old man said.

The deputy nudged a few small sticks with his boot.

"It couldn't be avoided," he said. "I thought I saw your grandson and his little buddy running out the back."

"So you was going to knock over my wood and chase them across Joe Hookstra's field?"

"You can file a grievance at the county office."

The old man pointed at the deputy's wet pants.

"You got a search warrant or did you piss all over that, too?" he said.

"We just want to ask Luke what he knows about Steve LaFrance's window getting shot out last night."

"There's a thousand people in this county that hate the son of a bitch more than Luke."

The deputy nodded. He looked out over the fields with his hand hovering by his pistol.

"I wish there was still some snow on the ground," he said. "I'd show you them tracks."

"I'm sure you could show me a lot of things," the old man said.

"Where's your grandson, Bruno?"

"You want to go inside or just gawk through the windows like a pervert?"

"I already made my surveillance."

"Survey up in them trees," the old man said. "Luke's probably hiding with them monkeys that fuck the birds."

Before sunrise the inductees at the military processing center in Chicago were stripped to their shorts and filed through a corridor longer than blocks of this city where for the first time Luke saw more buildings than sky. He and Adonis brought no underwear so the medical sergeants at the processing center gave them paper boxer shorts with a fly they tried holding shut. The walls were glassy with white paint and many boys leaned their cheeks against them and dozed in line with drool running from their mouths. They held paperwork attached to clipboards under their armpits.

Adonis spoke little and held a handful of waistband to keep his shorts around his gaunt hips. The paper had already torn along his leg. He was shivering, bumped like a plucked bird, and lifted his left foot before his right so that both feet never set on the cold tiles together. Luke studied the strange faces while the white-coated medical sergeants moved through the line promising that if the clipboards were lost, there would be no noon chow. The fat boys had worried eyes and held the clipboards with both hands. Adonis's teeth rattled from the cold. Luke looked at him perched upon one foot and shook his head before telling him to bone up.

"You get promoted or something?" Adonis said.

"You look like a fool," Luke said.

"Why should both my feet be cold?"

"Shit, Hill," Luke said. "You can't do things here that draw attention to yourself. These sergeants will make you pay for it."

"I ain't signed nothing yet."

"Go on and look like a dumbass."

"I will," Adonis said.

Luke turned back and stood rigidly along the wall. There were boys in line from the cornfields and he knew them by their broad shoulders from roofing jobs and their bleached white jockey shorts with nametags sewn into the waist-bands. There were also boys from the Indiana steel towns with faces like ore barges rusting in filthy rivers, their initials tattooed into forearms by sewing needles and india ink. The blacks laughed at everything and mostly kept to themselves. Some boys were big and violent-looking and flashed gang signs with contorted fingers. They mocked a jailhouse toughness that no teenager could truly understand and begged Luke to meet their eyes. He feigned reading through his paperwork, the forms where doctors deemed him fit or unfit for service, and silently decided which kids he could take in a fight. The poorest boys wore jockey shorts slit in the legs to make them fit, the cotton washed without bleach until sheer. A black kid with gel-wet hair break-danced in his leopard-spotted bikinis. He did the snake and moon-walked even after the line of inductees became bored and stopped watching.

The inductees were soon herderd into rooms that smelled of pine oil and paste wax. The dull-eyed sergeants ordered them to drop their shorts and aged doctors probed their rectums with gloved fingers and the boys closed eyes and ground teeth. The doctors squeezed testicles and told them to turn their heads and cough. They urinated in clear plastic cups. They gave vials of blood. Boys were asked if they ever cleaned ears, brushed teeth, did anything save smoke dope and watch television. Some were indifferently told they had heart murmurs, whooping coughs, stigmatisms, or flat feet. A fat boy from LaSalle County cried that he didn't need good feet to drive a tank. He even said that if they'd let him in the K9 Corps he would bring his own dog. "You don't walk there," he said. "The freaking dog does all the work." By noon Luke and Adonis were deemed fit for service and they enlisted in the United States Marine Corps as basic riflemen and swore to defend the Constitution of the United States for four years. The oath made some boys bleary-eyed but most only mouthed the words and looked like they were running off with the circus. Luke and Adonis were to report back in six days for shipment to the Marine Corps Recruit Depot, San Diego, California.

That afternoon they walked down Harrison Avenue toward the Greyhound station. They passed Greek lunch rooms where chickens roasted on long spits and the Chinese take-aways with steamed windows and burst mustard packets floating in the gutter water. The light rain fell slowly against the dark girders of the El tracks. Luke moved along the cracked sidewalk, staring at the gray sky, and thought the buildings were curling over the street like tree branches. They were transients in their Salvation Army clothes: sweatshirts from state colleges, blue jeans washed white and flecked with unknown fluids. Adonis stopped on the sidewalk and rerolled his jean cuff when a hard wind off Lake Michigan knocked him to his knees.

"Better put sandbags in your pockets," Luke said.

Adonis stood up. He turned and looked behind him. Dead

leaves scuttled along the sidewalk, a whirlwind of them, blowing between pools of lamplight in this early dusk.

"You couldn't have found any jeans shorter?" he said.

"You was standing right there."

"I found you a shirt that fit," Adonis said. "I made damn sure of it."

"Shit, Hill," Luke said. "I look like a bigger asshole than you do."

"I thought we'd be leaving for California in the morning. Them cops got us if we go home."

"The recruiter will be our alibi. He said it himself."

"That son of a bitch would have said anything."

"He didn't have to say that."

Adonis tried lighting a cigarette in the wind. He went through six matches before he got it going.

"When I come home on leave," Adonis said, "I'm going to the pool hall and smacking the shit out of some mother-fuckers."

"Whose ass you kicking first?"

"Any of them assholes. It don't matter."

Luke spat in the curb and laughed. Wet faces rolled past behind wet taxi windows. The blue motor smoke hung in the rain.

"I wonder if we'll run into Tim Ward," Luke said. "He's in San Diego. They took him after he got kicked out of high school for bringing a set of steak knives."

"He wouldn't claim us if we did. He's probably got fifty men under him by now. We'll have that many."

"Shit."

"They'll have to do anything we say. Even wash our clothes."

"What if they don't?" Luke said.

"I bet they got to stand there and take every one of our punches. We can kick them in the balls if we want."

"You don't know shit."

"They even got to say 'Thank you, sir, may I have another.'"

"You saw that in a movie," Luke said.

"But I bet it's like that."

"You feel good about this?" Luke asked.

"I don't feel bad," Adonis said. "But I do got a new respect for faggots. They got to be tough bastards for taking something up their asses all the time. That doctor's finger hurt like hell."

"You leave your paper underwear on?" Luke said.

"Fuck you, Konick."

They bought cigarettes for the ride home in a bodega across from the bus station and smoked outside beneath the small awning and looked at the rain in the street. Adonis studied himself in the storefront glass.

"You know what I hate?" he said.

"What."

"Walking around Chicago looking like this. It's embarrassing."

Luke looked at him and looked away.

"People would give you change if you asked them," he said.

"You don't look like much yourself."

"At least my jeans fit."

Adonis Hill grinned. "Come on," he said.

The Greyhound station was a long building fronted by windows, and half of them were boarded with plywood. They sat on high-backed wooden benches with their enlistment papers on the seats beside them and drank Cokes while the bus arrivals were announced over the intercom. There was a small lunch counter in the back where bums sat staring into ashtrays. The janitor was mopping the filthy tiles and the room smelled of pine oil. Luke looked at the name typewritten on Adonis's folder.

"Why the hell don't you go by Andrew?" he said. "You ain't fooling anybody with this Adonis shit."

"I'll be Andrew next week. Shit, then I guess I'll just be Hill. But in Watega I don't want nobody confusing me with a white boy."

"You are a white boy. I'd like to know how you come up with the name Adonis."

"Black people name all their kids stupid shit. But out in California, I'm going to be Mexican."

"Jesus Christ."

"Out there, Mexicans get special rights. All the towns are named for Mexicans. It's the thing to be."

"You don't got asthma either. They wouldn't have let you in."

"I just never wanted to run in PE class."

"What do you think you'll be doing next week?"

"The air's altogether different in California," Adonis said. "You don't even know you're running. It kind of soothes you."

Adonis stood and put his Coke can in the stand-up ash-tray.

"It don't go there," Luke said.

"You want another pop?"

"No."

"Piss on you," Adonis said. "I was buying."

The black kid sat down on the bench and watched Adonis stand and walk toward the Coke machine. He had cat's eyes that saw things even when he did not look upon them. He dropped his cigarette and left it burning on the wet floor. Luke and he met eyes like rival convicts. The kid blew two streams of smoke from his nose and nodded, then rose and pushed his way past old women with shiny handbags and boxes of fried chicken, fake fur coats, and sheer red head-scarves. Luke stood and took his hands from his pockets. The kid looked back at him every second step until he was beside Adonis and jerking the coin return on the pop machine like he'd lost money. Luke watched Adonis buy him a Coke and then give him a cigarette. Soon they talked and grinned like buddies. Adonis raised a finger and walked back over to Luke where he stood with his hand on the seat back.

"Sit your ass down and quit talking to people," Luke said.

"He's cool," Adonis said. "He wants to get me high for buying him a Coke."

The kid waited beneath the big station clock. He smoked the cigarette and French-inhaled over his thin lip. The windows bled from the rain.

"Sit down and wave him away," Luke said. "We ain't got but an hour."

"He's way cool."

"This ain't Watega."

"It's because he's black."

"That don't got anything to do with it. He looks screwy."

"That's you," Adonis said.

"Do what you're going to do," Luke said.

"I aim to."

Adonis and the kid went laughing up the stairs to the bathroom. They took the steps two at a time. The kid was lithe like a tom cat. Adonis looked thin and lost in his charity clothes. Luke started after them but stopped beneath the station clock while the intercom sounded a final boarding call for Toledo.

He ordered coffee from the station canteen and stood against the counter smoking and blowing steam off the paper cup. The counterman looked up warily from the sink. An old man gumming a cheeseburger watched the soap drip from his hands. The rain quickened in the street until the station windows blurred and buses parked along the curb became silver smears across the glass.

Luke was drinking the last of the coffee when the kid came running down the stairs with one hand deeply pocketed. He laughed out loud and the sound filled the station, but no one except Luke paid him any mind. Luke left his cigarette smoldering and made his way quickly from the counter without taking his change. The kid disappeared into the gray of Chicago but Luke kept looking for him while he climbed the steps. He'd been a flash, a piece of night. Outside there was nothing save the falling rain and a few Arab cab drivers stepping from their cabs to face Mecca and pray on the sidewalk.

Luke ran down the short hallway toward the sound of a running faucet. His heart was pounding and his mouth was dry. He made his way into the doorless restroom, ankle deep in paper towels, and tracked a puddle of urine across the brown tiles. Three of the six urinals were covered with visquine and the dried grime in the end sink was blood-splattered. He pushed the stall doors and called Adonis by name. He kicked at the one locked door until the latch rattled loose. His friend sat inside with his face in his hands.

"I thought he killed you the way he was running," Luke said.

Adonis did not look up. A thin stream of blood had clotted along his fingers.

"You cut bad?" Luke asked.

"He just touched me with it."

"Let me see."

Luke came closer and Adonis kicked at his knees.

"Let me see it," Luke said.

"He got me up here to suck his dick."

"We got to get you cleaned up," Luke said.

Adonis looked at the side of the stall. Someone had started tic-tac-toe with finger smears of feces.

"He had a knife on me, Luke," he said.

"Come on."

"You don't even think like yourself."

Luke looked at his watch.

"We got fifteen minutes," he said.

"He knew you wouldn't come up here," Adonis said. "But he knew I would. I got a look about me. I ain't going to last."

"Are you still bleeding?" Luke asked.

"It's like it wasn't even me when it was happening," Adonis said.

Luke reached out to touch him but he could not. He felt sick to his stomach. He stepped back and let the door swing halfway closed.

Bruno found the recruiting sergeant walking from the lunch counter at Woolworth's with a gape-mouthed boy, and his sea greens were marred from the rain. He followed them in his pickup the length of Court Street where last night half the parking meter heads were busted off with sledgehammers. They stopped in the recruiting office doorway and the sergeant lit a cigarette with a Zippo shinier than his shoes. The boy had a bad tick, his face quaking like a cat trying to vomit. Bruno parked against the curb where the glass from the meters sparkled. His hand trembled on the gearshift with a cigarette between his fingers after he shut down the truck. He held his hand still upon his knee and rolled down the window, waiting for the right time to call this marine a son of a bitch. *I bet you ran some good bullshit on Luke, you jarhead asshole.* "You

*join my Marine Corps, kid, I'll take you home and let you
screw my sister."*

The sergeant patted the boy's feeble back like they were
comrades who shared the same hooker. The boy wore
denim and flannel, faded from work and washing. The
sergeant gave the boy a cigarette and lit it.

"All you got to do is put in seventy-five dollars a month," he
said. "The Marine Corps will match it two to one. After four
years, you'll have eighty-one hundred dollars for college."

The boy ticked and wiped drool from his mouth corners.

"I got this .22 Winchester I can really shoot with," he said. "I
hit a rabbit in the head when it was coming out of some weeds
by the creek. I was wondering if I can bring it with me."

"You'll learn to fire the M-16," the sergeant said.

"But I might not be able to shoot with it too good."

"The Marine Corps will teach you."

"I already know on my .22 Winchester. I've had it since I
was eight years old. I figure they could make me a special
sniper."

"We'll teach you better on the M-16."

"You think so?" the boy said.

"I know it."

The boy snuffled loudly.

Bruno leaned his face out the window into the rain. He
was ready to call the sergeant a goddamned liar, a Vietnam
marine whose medals were consolation prizes and so worth-
less they would not get him a donut and coffee in trade. The
kid looked up at the sergeant with confused eyes, amazed
that anybody would want him to belong to anything. Bruno
sat quietly in the truck while the sergeant opened the door
and led the boy inside. He'd paid Bruno no mind at all, perhaps figuring this was one more old man waiting on Jack
Brosseau at the Rexall drugstore to fill his prescription for
gout medication. Bruno stared at the cardboard marine with
the glinting saber lifted between his eyes in full salute. The
storefront window was slow to fill with rain. *"Anywhere but
here, Sergeant,"* Luke probably said. *"It just don't matter."*

* * *

The wind shredded the country when he was gone. Barn shingles lay scattered in the road and the sticks from hedgerows a mile away tangled with the roadside grass. Across his lane the dead hickory was down and broken three ways, the barkless wood white as cold moonlight. The mailbox floated in the brown ditch water amongst bird nests and crushed beer cans. He parked the truck and walked up the lane. The clapboards from his house were strewn across the front yard, wound with pink insulation. A flock of starlings flapped above him as if a dark wave. *Son of a bitch.*

Smoke rose straight and thick from the toolshed chimney. He walked there and his dogs eyed him stonily from their shacky house and the lantern light was splayed and near glowless in the shed windows. Without knowing why, he imagined the dead moths smoldering in the lamp, the soot rising as if spilling upwards. Len stood inside with his back to the window, working a chamois over the bare metal Whizzer frame where it hung from two straightened coat hangers. He wore the old man's coveralls and talked slowly as if explaining the work to an apprentice. The lantern light made the newsprint papering the wall look like it bubbled and rose to a head. He rubbed a while, then ceased, pointing at the metal where the chamois had touched and lecturing himself. The old man watched the lantern flame like a frightened dog before turning from the bad glass. *I knew right what would ruin you and there was nothing I could do because this world don't make allowances for men who feel too much.*

The shed door opened and Len wrung his hands and looked at Bruno while he glanced about. He nodded toward the tire ruts where the old man usually parked his pickup.

"Where's your truck?" Len asked.

"I parked on the road," Bruno said. "The wind put that dead hickory right across the lane."

The old man pointed off at the yard filled with sticks and clapboards. He kept seeing Len talking to himself.

"It all happened since you been gone," Len said.

"You hear it real good?" Bruno said.

"I was here in the middle of it."

The old man pocketed his hands.

"You find Luke?" Len asked.

"I think the marines got him. If he took the oath, he took it. A boy his age got to feel a thing with his ass before he believes it's true."

"You're done now?" Len said.

The old man walked down the lane toward the barkless tree glowing in the quarterdarkness. Len followed him past a heap of rusted farm implements.

"I'll let you know when I need help with the tree," Bruno said.

"I'm sorry for the Depression," Len said. "I'm sorry that Grandpa was too sick to work and I'm sorry for World War II. But you got to quit punishing us for it."

"I can't save a goddamned thing," Bruno said.

The old man turned away from his son and those eyes huge and blue and wanting.

Luke and Adonis made their way down the bus aisle where anonymous sleepers dozed chin to chest and past the driver who stared at his busted nose in the windshield. The small parking lot was empty and the wind blew their bangs across their faces and the puddles riffled from the wind and pooled the yellow light from the little station windows. Adonis watched the bus doors slam shut before it drove toward the interstate exit on Court Street. His eyes looked after it like he left something on the vinyl seats. They stood quiet for a while, the night a hazy pitch without stars above the squat houses and the river and the empty country. Behind the station windows, the dark figure of a man mopping passed before the glass like a shooting-gallery bear. Luke looked up the street where Adonis was staring, but there was nothing to see.

"We could stay at my house in town," he said.

"You been there since your dad died?" Adonis asked.

"No."

"There any heat?"

"There's blankets."

"I ain't going to sleep where no man killed himself," Adonis said.

"He didn't do it in the house."

"I still ain't."

"Where the hell you going to stay?"

"I don't know. I ain't tired enough for it to be important."

They walked to the street and leaned their stomachs against a parked car. The river spooled between the clapboard houses like moving ground. Adonis kept his face down the way he had the whole ride back from Chicago. Luke rested his elbows on the car roof and smelled rain in the night even though it quit long before dusk.

"My dad knew Skinny real good," Luke said. "I bet he'll let us drink beer if we show him our enlistment papers."

"I don't got no money."

"I've been keeping some back just for this."

"I didn't even have any for that nigger to steal," Adonis said.

"I got six bucks. That's six schooners a piece plus what Skinny will buy us for joining the marines."

"How do you know he'll sell you shit?" Adonis said.

"Veterans figure that if you can shoulder a rifle for America, you can drink a beer."

"That ain't what the law says."

"Sometimes laws aren't right."

Luke took Adonis by the arm but he pulled away. He stood there silent and ruined in his blood-stained windbreaker.

"I told you I was buying," Luke said.

"That ain't it."

"I'll never say anything about it. We're buddies forever now."

"You ain't even listening to me," Adonis said.

"I don't know what I would've done if I was you."

"You would have killed that son of a bitch or died yourself."

"I don't know that."

"But I do," Adonis said. "And so will everybody who ever looks at me."

"Shit, Hill. Who's going to know?"

"You will," Adonis said. "We ain't equals no more."

Luke was silent. He put a cigarette in his mouth and fished about his pockets for a match. The river ran high from the rains and he heard the current against the bridge piers at Washington Avenue. Adonis took his enlistment papers from the folder and set them on the wet car roof. The folder scuttled down the street and the papers blew off the roof like birds taking to flight. Adonis said nothing and started down the street. Luke smoked while Adonis faded off into the darkness and thought that any time he would stop and turn back, but he never did. Soon Luke stood alone in the gutter water that ran with the force of a rivulet. He walked off the other way and headed for Station Street where the neon beer signs always left streaks of colored light in the tavern windows.

Luke was soaked from the old rain that blew off the oak trees when he stood in the doorway of Skinny's Tap. He stomped his shoes and wiped the cold water from his eyes. The horseshoe bar was filled with women in snagged bikini tops and matching red thongs and they rubbed the backs of men still filthy from foundry work. They had fat on their shoulders, tattooed backsides, thighs like big logs gone to termites. Luke closed the door and crossed to the bar and stood at the fake wood counter while men poured whiskey shots into beer schooners and drank from the bowled glasses with wide eyes. A little man sat across the bar and his belly spilled from a blue work shirt. Two women stroked his acne-scarred cheeks with chubby hands while they danced and their butt cheeks shook on either side of the thong. He was buying carnival tickets to keep the women's hands on him, twenty dollars worth, and they snatched his money right off the bar.

It was redlit in the tavern from the Christmas lights wound over the barback mirror. Luke was looking up from a calendar picture of the Iwo Jima Memorial taped over the bottle necks when the bartender eyed him hard. He shook his pinched face.

"I ain't even going to ask for your ID," he said.

"I just want a beer," Luke said.

"You ain't allowed in here to even ask."

Luke showed his enlistment papers like a poker hand.

"I joined the marines today," he said. "These here are my papers. I figured I could drink beer since I'm leaving next week."

The bearded man beside Luke laughed out loud. Smoke fell from his nose in thin streams. He shook cold the match that lit his cigarette.

"You eighteen?" the man said to Luke.

"Yessir."

"Get the kid a Coke, Butch," he said. "And get me a double shot of Early Times."

The bartender squinted through the smoke streaming from the ashtrays.

"It'll be on me," the man said.

"You bet your ass it will," the bartender said.

The man pushed two dollars into the well while the bartender poured the whiskey and the Coke. He waved away two women with creased thighs before they even crossed the cracked floor. Luke reached into his pockets.

"You can't pay here," the man said. "Now drink the whiskey and chase her back with that pop."

Luke took the double shot, a slow burn, then sipped off the Coke. Two fat women danced by the jukebox, the ticket rolls in their hands like pistols. The man waited for him to swallow.

"My name's Tom McCracken," he said. "Fifth Marines. Semper Fi, Mac."

Luke didn't answer. He looked at the man and wondered what to say.

"That's how jarheads introduce themselves," the man said.

"I'm Luke Konick. My dad drank here."

The man nodded.

"We was over there about the same time," he said. "I used to tell Bruce how lucky he was. Then I quit even talking to him."

"I ain't thinking about him no more," Luke said.

"Sometimes remembering is harder than forgetting."

"I was wondering if you knew what them men are buying the tickets for?" Luke said.

"They raffle off lap dances later."

"I don't know what you mean, sir," Luke said.

The man grinned and blew smoke across the bar.

"It's where a girl sits on your lap and humps you with her crotch," he said.

"They do that for money?"

"Later on they'll do worse than it. Right back in the pool room."

"Skinny's retired navy," Luke said. "I wouldn't think he'd let this fly."

"He brings the girls down from Joliet in his van."

"Shit," Luke said. "I always thought this was a place where veterans talked to each other."

"Who the hell do you think are buying the tickets?"

"I never thought I'd see this in here," Luke said.

"What do you think being a veteran is?"

"I don't know."

"It ain't sitting around the Legion hall telling stories," the man said. "It's more like a night that don't end."

"What do you mean?"

"I can't put it to you any other way," the man said.

Luke folded his enlistment papers. He did it slowly and with care.

Len and the old man sat at the table drinking coffee and smoking when Luke came home. The morning was dark and it had snowed in the night, the white outline starkly visible upon the fell hickory branches. The old man took his tinware cup to the sink and slung the grounds down the drain and went to the stovetop and filled the cup from a cast iron pot and came back to the table. He passed Luke twice, close enough to get a good smell, but said nothing. On the table was a plate of fried ham and white bread in a bag and Tabasco sauce. Luke washed his hands in the sink and dried them with a rag towel and sat down at the table. The old man stirred his coffee even though he took it black and read last night's paper without his glasses. Luke made a sandwich and doused the ham with Tabasco and salt. The old man peered over the newspaper at him.

"Looks like the bear bit you real good," he said. "But not so bad you don't got enough ass to sit on."

Luke set down the sandwich already bitten and lifted the bread and poured on some more Tabasco. Len spooned two scoops of sugar into his coffee and left the spoon in his cup and pushed back in his chair. He knew this game well, how the old man beat you calmly with insults and reduced you with his glare until you shriveled like fried bacon or lost your temper. It was best to stay quiet because you were judged weak for not fighting, but the moment you fought back he only quietly shook his head as if you were too emotional to be a man at all. Luke chewed and rolled his eyes like he knew this game as well and was bored by it.

"So you went and did it," the old man said.

"I joined the marines up in Chicago," Luke said, "but I didn't kill nobody the way you make it sound."

"It ain't going to be no dickdance."

"I'm eighteen."

"You sure the hell are," the old man said.

"There ain't nothing wrong with me."

"I was agreeing with you, boy. Just finish that sandwich because you're earning it back on the river today. We're going after some trees."

Luke snarled and dropped the sandwich on the bare wooden table.

"Go on, lose your temper," the old man said. "But you're not laying around my house like the hero you think you're going to be."

"I didn't say anything about being a hero," Luke said.

"These are the rules," the old man said. "You buy the ham and heating oil and I might consider your opinion. But I ain't even going to ask you about shooting out a cop's back window."

Luke hit the table with his knee when he stood and walked to the back of the house. Len heard the closet door open and shoes hitting the walls. The old man pushed his plate forward into the Tabasco bottle and its edge chinked against the heavy glass ashtray. Len looked out the window. The trees were only etchings upon the starless dark. The old man made a whisking, dismissal motion with his hand. He drank his coffee slowly so that Len could see the movements of his pleated throat.

"Them DIs will read that little asshole his rights," he said.

"You don't have to be this way to him," Len said.

"What way? Give him ham for breakfast and make him work a bit?"

"We didn't do it to you," Len said.

The old man was up from his chair and looking at Len with hot eyes.

"You want to smack the shit out of me and end this?" he said. "I won't even hit you back."

Len sat at the table and watched his father put his hands in his back pockets and stand a minute as if something wild. *You're not the man I was shit scared of. You can't even stand up against a wind anymore.*

The sky was a slate of grayish black without clouds when they drove off in the morning. Len sat by the window and Luke was beside him while the old man headed east toward the dawn paling over the river bend. Axes and oiled blades for the chainsaw and the gas cans rattled against the grooved bed of the pickup truck. Soon the country appeared white and aglow with frost and the new light glinted the furrows and the hedge trees, and the fencepost shadows fell sideways upon the snowy mud like railroad tracks. Their boots were already wet from the frost off the grass.

The old man turned down a rutted tractor road and Luke feigned sleep with his head nodding chin to chest. A landscape of whiteboard houses and barns long void of stock and hay stood beyond the town limits. Back west the light of the fallen stars showed vaporous from below the horizon and Len watched it dissolve into the coming morning. The old man hit a deep rut and the chains slid around the bed and knocked the gas cans to their sides. Luke's neck jerked straight. "Son of a bitch," he said.

"I thought I told you to tie them chains off," the old man said. "Them cans, too."

Luke did not open his eyes.

"I did," he said. "I tied them together."

"That makes no shitting sense. You were supposed to tie them off to something."

"Off to what?"

"Any goddamned thing. The rail along the sides. The frigging toolbox."

The old man drove on. The axes slid and gonged against the gate. He looked at Luke and snarled and shook his head, then stopped the truck in a copse of weeds while two rabbits went shooting down the furrows.

"My nerves are about slid out of my mouth," he said. "If you pull this shit in the Marine Corps, you'll be double-timing with them axes over your head until your arms give out."

"I don't think I'll be cutting down trees," Luke said.

"You don't even know, boy," the old man said. "Come next week the world and a shitstorm are going to look exactly the same."

The old man stopped the truck and shifted down to neutral and pulled the brake. He got out and Len watched him cuss and spit in the snow. They must have smelled spilled gas at the same time because the old man pulled off his hat and threw it against the back window. He showed teeth and breathed hard, then tied the tools and the gas cans to the rails with greasy rope. Len looked at Luke, his eyes still closed.

"I ain't even interested," Luke said.

"There were things that happened," Len said.

"Listen, you freak son of a bitch. None of us believe my dad fucked you up the ass. And if you got something to prove to the old man, just wait until I'm gone to do it."

Before Len could answer the old man was back in the

truck and pulling the door closed. His cap was smudged with dirty snow. He popped the brake and put the truck in gear.

"Them DIs will rip your balls off and fry them with onions," the old man said to Luke.

"You think? Then maybe Lenny should come with me. He might like it fine."

"Just let one catch you being a dumbass," the old man said.

"You talk like you've had your balls ripped off and fried."

"No sir. In my day the krautheads just killed you dead and kept on moving."

Luke sat up and opened his eyes red and bleary from sleeplessness.

"You don't think I've got balls enough," he said.

"The dumbest dog God ever made has balls."

"You send my dad off this way?" Luke said.

Silence fell inside the cab. All Len heard was the tires popping over the ruts. Luke smiled and closed his eyes.

The country was plain in the way of its whiteboard churches and all things were replicas of the last sight beheld until Len thought the truck ceased movement. In the air were flurries and the fumed smoke from farmers' trash fires. Nothing abided here except the miles of wire fence and hedge and the fields that spent half the year as scars. They passed a limestone quarry flooded with slattern water and the old man turned down a craggy road and headed for the bottom fields. He looked as if he saw something coming out of the long emptiness the way his stare was unbroken through the windshield. Len blew warmth into his bare hands and searched the country for what his father might be seeing, but found nothing.

The old man parked the truck and they gathered the tools and walked down through the woods while the white sun shone in the branches. The flurries reeled through the bare limbs and dusted the shaded deadfall. Len followed the old man down the hill with the ropes and the topping spikes and the river grew wider through the black trees. The old

171

man carried the chainsaw like a suitcase. Luke lagged behind with the axes and the gas cans.

The old man stopped in matted weeds where deer had lain for the night. Len waited for his father to point this out, but he only set down the saws in the shadows from three oaks and studied the branches where they interlocked and patted the tree he wanted to cut first. Len dropped the topping spikes and came over to see. They lit cigarettes and stood listening to Luke kick at rotten deadwood. The tree was the tallest oak with long limbs winding about the trunks of the smaller trees so that if it was cut without first being topped, nothing that morning would fall right.

Luke came down the slope to lean against a hickory and smoke. The axes lay up the hill where he dropped him. The snow gathered in his hair. The old man looked at him and pulled his cap low so that his eyes were shaded.

"What are them axes doing in the mud?" he said. "The fricking trees are down here."

Luke blew smoke and cold, then spat.

"I figured you was going to smoke and look around at everything for a good twenty minutes," he said.

"You didn't answer me."

"There's still fifteen minutes left for you to see something different than last week," Luke said.

The old man shook his head and looked out where the sunlight lay broken on the water. He bit off a plug of tobacco. Len unslung the coiled rope from his shoulder and the old man took the end and tied it off to the chainsaw handle and then buckled the topping spikes over his muddy boots and ran the safety belt around his waist and the oak trunk. Len reached forward and checked the clamp and the D-ring.

"I can do this," he said.

"You ever climbed a tree on spikes?"

"No."

"What makes you think you can do it?" the old man said.

"I watched you a thousand times."

"Just stand away and keep an eye on that little asshole up

the hill. I hope the marines got a shot for a bad case of the dumbass."

The old man took the rope end in his teeth and with a violent gouge set the left spike deep into the tree and then came the right a bit higher and soon the rope unwound from the coil and he was climbing the trunk. He stopped below the first branch and inched his way left, the spikes rising and staving hard into the oak. The limbs swayed from the wind and their shadows fell across his face. Len watched him look at the river and the yellow limestone dells along the far bank and looked himself, wondering what his father always saw, when the old man began pulling up the chainsaw hand over hand. Luke sat in the sun with closed eyes and drug his cigarette.

Blackbirds jumped from the thickets when he fired the saw and flew across the river in a thin, dark line. A crow circled in the widening sunlight and dropped close to the water where the flurries left splash rings atop the current. He leaned back in the safety belt, stiff-legged and very dark in his clothes. He set the saw against the limb and the teeth chewed through knots and frozen sap while the arc of wood splinters spun against his face.

Where the branch had once been, the sunlight came sleek and brutal. The old man wielded the saw against another branch as if the spinning blade had become his thoughts. He eyed the cuts he made. The branches fell all around him, the dry sticks goring the snow, the limbs quaking over skeletal scrub bushes and splashing into the river. Soon the tree was stripped and the fell wood lay about like the appendages of a slain beast. He shut down the saw. He studied where the wood dust had settled in the leaf-strewn washes while the smoke from the saw dispersed in the sunlight. The snow turned into flakes. He looked coldly upon the wreckage like he saw other things.

After the old man climbed down the trunk, he walked over to Luke in his spikes. Two crows flew spanning their vile wings and gliding off into the snow. Luke leaned against a tree and watched the crows as if forecasting their flight direction. The old man kicked his boot.

"You better learn to stand your ass up real fast before next week," he said.

"Shit," Luke said.

"Your bowels will be so tight you won't take one the first two weeks of boot camp."

"And I'll think of you when it finally busts loose."

"Just go up the hill and make some coffee. Try not to piss off the rabbits."

Luke rose sneering and headed up the slope. He cursed to himself and flipped the old man off when he turned around.

Len heard the dogs long before they jumped the deadfall on the limestone ridge in a tight, dark wedge. Their barking echoed like shotgun reports through the whitelit wood. The old man looked up from filling his pipe from a sandwich bag of tobacco. Far below the dogs, the deer they trailed went sideways down the slope with an arrow in its hind, bent-legged and very brown against the autumnal sun. The old man took off his hat and spat while the boy squatted on the hilltop and broke sticks over his knee.

The young deer did not want to cross the creek. When he did, the dogs had gained on him. He came all slick and quaking from the cattails on the bank and started for the thicket. Behind him the dogs were jumping down into the creek wildly and the water erupted about them. While they crossed, their long black hair shrank against their bony haunches, and when they came out of the water into the glade, they came among wisps of cold breath.

The deer did not veer until the lead dog reached the thicket. By now the blood pumped from the arrow wound and he was slowing. He righted and swung his rack at the dog and loped into the shadows. The dogs flanked from the scrub and brier and swarmed over his forelegs and he twisted and stabbed with his few points and reared back on his wounded hind when his haunches gave way. He collapsed with his front legs raised, buried in a tribe of baying dogs

until he caught the lead's neck with his rack and struck
upon it and raised and impaled the dog. When he turned to
defend his throat, he could not.

The old man took up an ax to scare off the hounds and
started for the creek where amid the yelps the wounded dog
had slunk off into the water. Len watched him slow his
approach to a solemn walk, then stop in the sunlit flurries,
as if to receive a blessing, or to confer one. He motioned Len
forward with the ax but Len would not come see. His father
smiled like a man finally proven right.

From the ridge Luke was looking down upon the killing
in terror and soon turned away to set the sticks one by one
in the kindling fire, and the flames hissed and guttered. The
deer lay dead with wide black eyes and the wounded dog
quaked in the cold creek and raised its snout to let go thin,
baleful howls, the throat blood pooling on a skein of leaves
until the animal folded into the water and died. Len hugged
the topped oak, the cut rings wet, and cried silently while
his father took a knee and watched the dogs tear horribly at
the deer's neck and fling gore and tissue against the tree
trunks. *You are, father, what you have always been. I can only
see you the way I want you to be when I am looking away.*

The smoke from the boy's fire rose thinly through the
branches because there was no wind on the hill where he
squatted breaking the limbs and watching the sky. Len saw
that his fire was vague in the hard white sunlight.

The oak rounds lay in the orchard shadows. Their weight left black scratches on the snow when the old man rolled them into the open with his boot. He kicked one flat and it set heavy before sinking down in the grass. The snow lined the furrows along the field breaks and weeds bowed from the wind and the snow blew into his eyes. Many logs had spilled over the truck gate on the way home because they loaded them quickly and not right, rushing ahead of the storm. He sent Len and the boy back down the Saint Marie blacktop because he was sure they left a trail of wood. They finished rolling the rounds from the truck bed and drove off without looking at each other. Their eyes were running from the cold.

The clouds formed to the west like rimrock mountains. His heart burned as if it would sear through his breast bone.

He leaned on the ax and drew troubled breath. The pain first came when he heard the hunter's whistles calling the dogs off the deer in the creek and back the way of their harrying. The dead dog sank beneath the skein of leaves, his throat blood diluted in the cold water. When the hunters appeared upright and armed with long bows, bearded men in camouflage and day-glo, the dogs heeled on the bank and shook with joy. The hunters spat and eyed the mauled deer and the carcass of their dog while the wind swept the river to swells, paying Len and the old man no mind at all. Without gesture, they turned and left the animals dead in the mud, as if the sight was not worth the sunlight cast upon it, and returned back upcountry with the dogs trotting behind slumpnecked and smeared with gore.

The old man worked through the hour while the grass turned white in the back pasture. He split the rounds into pieces and stacked them against the fence before he shouldered the ax and went back across the grass into the orchard shadows. A round lay dusted with snow and he eyed it where his ax would first hit, then spat a gout of tobacco juice. But this time his hands were slow to grip the worn handle and the blade landed flat when it struck the wood. He blew into his palms and worked his fingers as if casting a spell. The ax dropped away when his hands would not close. His left eye twitched and went numb as did his face. The blood slowed through his body. He gasped and staggered backward and leaned against a cherry tree and the thin branches cradled him. The snow fell silently. To him, the air was neither cold nor warm. The dogs called from their pen and the old man slid downward. He let his eyes close and thought he heard birds.

The dogs howled without pause while his uncle reversed the truck back to the woodpile. Luke saw the old man in the sideview mirror, curled beneath the cherry tree where snow had gathered upon his back. He opened the door and went running into the snow before his uncle stopped the truck. The wind trapped fifteen starlings and the birds flew in circles above the orchard. Luke reeled from the same wind and slipped twice. The old man lay in the snow drawing breath faintly, his hands blue from the cold, the ax dropped beside him. He opened his eyes when Luke knelt over him, looking up through eyelids like crescent moons. His lips quivered when he tried speaking. Luke held the old man's head and snowflakes melted upon his lips.

"You hear me?" Luke said.

The old man's eyes closed when he raised his right hand.

His jeans were stiff with frozen mud. The hand fell fanwise into a snow-filled bootprint. Luke felt his throat and the slow pulse within. His breath came as if mist against glass.

"Jesus," Luke said.

He kept the old man's pulse with two fingers and called for his uncle, but found him standing against the tree with snowflakes slamming into his face. Len was dazed, watching the starlings reel until one gust scattered the flock and the white haze engulfed their tiny wings.

"We got to get him up," Luke said.

Len sat down against a cherry tree. He drew his knees in and hugged himself. Breath came hard and fitful from his nose. He grabbed his shoulders and looked at Luke and leaned slowly back until cradled by the thin branches. He closed his eyes. Luke held the old man's head with both hands.

"You son of a bitch," he said.

Len did not move. The snow rose about his outstretched legs.

"You freak son of a bitch," Luke said.

He steadied himself and coughed and got his breath. The old man's hair hung in slick gray locks. A blue vein swelled from his forehead. Luke clenched his teeth and took hold under the old man's armpits and lifted him to his feet. His uncle darkened like the sky out west.

They stood together while the dogs lunged against the pen and the old man drew air through a lone nostril. Luke's breath plumed and he wrapped his arms around the old man's chest and pulled him close. He whispered that his night had not yet fallen. He swore that he would not let death take his last father and then kissed his grandfather's cold neck and tasted sawdust. Snow gathered in Len's hair the way it did along the thin cherry branches and he sat with his face in his hands. Luke started backward for the truck and the snow filled the cuts made by his grandfather's boots. The dogs went silent and took the scent by throwing back their snouts and soon lay down to cry. He sat the old man in the truck seat and drove off with his wet head in his lap.

He kept to the middle of the road because the snow was drifting across the barditch. The blue of the Saint Marie water tower was hardly visible and the storm smeared the tree line along the Watega River. The old man's breath filled with phlegm and he drooled snot on Luke's jeans and his legs were slanted and curled upon the floor mat. Luke talked out loud. He stroked his grandfather's forehead and the sweat turned colder. The tires slipped on the county roads and the truck veered while Luke turned the wheel against the wind. He told the old man he loved him and cried hard enough to blur the country and soon the breath slowed against his hand. His grandfather was silent. Luke leaned on the gas pedal and counted pulse beats.

Three hours later he was sitting in the surgical waiting room at Saint Mary's Hospital. He was filthy from the river and his boots had printed all of the tiles between the water fountain and the chair. It was only him and the fat nurse, but he heard voices and the sounds of carts with bum wheels moving through the long corridors. Her round, kind face made him angry and he did not know why. She looked at him like he was a stray animal and he stared at the table of magazines until she walked back to her station. He sat back and crossed his legs straight before him and half remembered the old man slipping from his red hands outside the emergency room while the wet snow squalled across the car hoods in the parking lot. But it seemed a long time ago. He'd seen the old nun with button-black eyes pointing the way from behind the reception desk with a scoured hand. There was the crucifix above a row of chairs and the gift shop was closed and the fluorescent light fumed in the waxed floor tiles and held upside down a blurred likeness of the cross. The elevator bell rang when the doors parted for no one at all. He drug the old man from under his armpits and stood reeling by the nun. He saw the darkness roll slowly beneath his eyeballs. Don't go down, he told himself.

But he had. What sobered him was two black orderlies lifting the old man to a gurney and covering the mud and wood dust of his clothes with a sheet. Luke lay in the narrow hallway, propped up against the wall, screaming while his eyes focused. A Chinese doctor in gym shoes and surgical scrubs was patting his cheek. He seized the man's strong wrist and looked up into his face and knew his eyes were darting. The doctor did not try to pull away and instead came closer and said a dozen words very fast. Luke understood none of it and started telling the man what he knew. *"He's worse than the way I found him. He got cold on the drive in from Saint Marie and couldn't crack his eyes no more. He's a smoker. The son of a bitch really likes to smoke."*

Luke spat in the wastebasket and motioned to the fat nurse that he was going outside for a smoke. He put two fingers to his lips very quickly. "Down by them electric doors," he said before she asked. She smiled sadly from behind the desk and they both looked at the clock, as if in the time would be revealed the old man's fate. He rose and rode the elevator down to the lobby where the nun sat behind the reception desk, her ropy hands quietly turning newspaper pages, her black sweater held closed by a toothpick. *"He must have been having small strokes all year,"* the doctor told him. *"There is much damage to his heart and he did not know what was happening to him."*

Luke went outside the electric doors and lit a cigarette and stood smoking it with one boot jacked against the wall. A semi was halted for the storm on Court Street, a block before the river bridge, and the trailer had slid sideways on the ice. The headlights blinked against the darkness and illuminated snow in long cones. The box shape of the trailer was nearly invisible as was the river eddying around the bridge piers. The driver's silhouette flashed red while he lit flares and laid them on the lane lines. The wind drove the snow and shook the stop sign at the entrance to the parking lot. When the flares dulled, the man and his shadow were gone.

The snow was drifting in the bands of streetlight when Luke walked off across the parking lot. Through the squall, the truck existed without the town giving background or the brown river coursing beneath the bridge. He walked into the blizzard and felt scared and alone and at once all things seemed entities lost unto themselves, as if the nearness of men and their lives were an exaggeration of proximity the way stars from a constellation showed very close together on summer nights. He was afraid for this lone driver and called out some greeting that was lost to the snow and the distance. The reply was also lost to the storm, if it came at all.

There was now ice in the wind and it beat Luke's face and sounded against the parked cars. He headed back for the hospital and moved among the shadows cast by the lot lights when he saw the nun pallid and hunched with a lone hand holding her sweater closed. She stood in the doorway and stared vacantly, not at him, not at the storm. Luke sprinted and twice the iced cement brought him to his knees, and after falling a third time he rose and ran past the nun.

The doctor stood by the table of magazines when the elevator doors opened. He played with the button of his pen and his white tennis shoes were stained with bile. Before Luke even cleared the foyer by the elevator, the doctor told him that the old man arrested twice while they were closing. His face was pinched and he clicked the pen hard, then looked at his watch. Luke saw that he was angry and did not want to explain himself.

"Is he dead?" Luke asked.

"If you want to see him with a pulse," the doctor said, "you better go in now."

"It ain't going to be him," Luke said.

The doctor rolled his eyes and looked down the hallway. He eyed his watch again, then the clock above the nurse's station, comparing the times. He turned off down the hallway and glanced at Luke over his shoulder, already walking through the blurred bands of light in the tiles.

"The nurse will show you the way," he said.

"Hey doctor," Luke said.

"Go in and see him."

"I need you to tell me something."

"It's okay," the doctor said. "Go in and see him."

"It ain't okay," Luke said. "Nothing's okay."

The doctor stopped and sighed and did not turn his face to talk.

"I came back to revive him," he said. "I was in my car. I was driving away when I got paged."

Luke watched him walk off and drag his pen along the cinderblock walls, cursing under his breath. He was a disgusted man. The hallway smelled of pine oil and cafeteria food. He followed the nurse with his hands pocketed and passed the darkened rooms where the neatly made beds glowed. His baseball cap was low over his eyes. The nurse sucked a breath mint.

The light turned grainy beyond the doors of the intensive care unit. There was a row of beds where the anesthetized men lay shrouded in paper gowns. Some wore fresh bandages inside their thighs where the surgeons took veins to replace the clogged arteries around their hearts. They slept the dreamless sleep of drunks. Upon their legs were the old yellowed scars from the beaches at Normandy and Saipan and many wore the mottled tattoos from that war. Hearts run through with knives. Hissing snakes. The Marine Corps globe and anchor. Luke heard the respirator when they neared the old man and the nurse pointed the way around the curtain. While he walked he also heard the wind. He stopped and listened to it. So faint, as if night breath. He could feel the cold seeping and he watched the snow twist through the window light before it leaned out into the darkness.

The nurse smiled at him when he looked back, then walked away. He listened to the beep he knew was his grandfather's life. His stomach sank fast enough to knock him down and he steadied himself with his hand against the

THE NAMES OF RIVERS

railing of a vacant bed. He stepped quickly behind the curtain as if jumping into cold water.

In his field jacket he stood and watched the heart monitor's dark screen. The green line and the image of the green line mirrored in his eyes bent and smeared when the heart beat sound, and again after he closed his eyes to dream himself the wind. He left his hands in his pockets and came slowly forward. He looked down at the tiles dulling from the snow off his boots. His fingers tinted green when he held his hand to the monitor light. He looked at the face so pale and waxen on the hospital pillow. The plastic tube filled the old man's lungs with air and his entire body trembled when they deflated. *The whole fucking thing is hardly a dream. Hardly a dream.*

The small backhoe was loaded on the trailer across the cemetery near the wrought-iron gate. The bucket held cold dirt from his father's grave and Len had watched it fill with snow throughout the reading of the Psalms. The young priest wore a black wool cape over his vestments and the wind lifted the train past his shoulders while he turned the pages in the prayer book after having lost his place. The old men held old women by the arms and they bowed their heads and the gusts knocked over folding chairs beneath the small awning and the snow disappeared into their hats and coats. Len was standing looking at the bare oaks and past the cemetery at the fog of snow along the horizon. He knew the boy was not coming nor would he ever come again. The priest raised his small hands in benediction and they trembled from the cold as did his lips and while he spoke the wind surged and the oak branches beat together. *Enter, rejoice, and come in. Today will be a joyful day. Enter, rejoice, and come in.* Len bowed his head and received the final blessing. The old men without wives gathered on the road and slouched beside their pickups and drank whiskey chased with the mouthfuls of snow they scraped off the truck hoods.

The priest finished and asked all to go in peace and walked away from the casket with two humpbacked widows. He carried a prayer book and a rosary was wound about its spine and the crucifix turned and turned again when the flakes hit it. The widows each held the priest's arm as if he were their bridegroom and the mourners headed back to their cars and left folding chairs where they lay in the snow. Len stood alone watching the casket turn the flakes into dirty water. He looked at his mother's gravestone beaded with the same water and told the wind that he only dreamed six times about her when he was a boy until all the dreams became one and her memory left him forever. The old men drank by the road and laughed through stories about his father. The cigar smoke fumed from their mouths as if they were horses working in the cold. Len soon followed the fresh footprints out of the cemetery and the drunk men stared at him with a confused silence and perhaps thought they looked upon the younger ghost of the man they buried. Some smiled sadly with wet eyes, maybe seeing back forty years when they met up in barrooms that autumn of 1945 to see who was left. Jack Wisnowsky turned away from Len and looked out at the country and sucked snot back through his nose.

The mourners drove to Bertrand's Café in a long line of pickup trucks when the funeral was over. The noon seemed as if dusk were upon the country. Len parked at the curb outside the dollar theater where barn pigeons nested in the marquee, and walked up the sidewalk with the wind reddening his face. The streetlights already shined their faint yellow and the nights now would come early and be long and aglow with snow and moon.

Len waited for a long time outside the diner. Out in the street the snow slashed through the gray fog and vanished into the standing water pooled around the sewer grates. He nodded to old men while they closed truck doors and shook the sleet from their hats. The diner windows fogged with smoke and breath and he vaguely saw Art Bertrand setting platters of baloney and ham on the counter beside greasy buckets of chicken. His hands were shaking. The old men pulled six-packs of beer from brown bags wet from snow and wiped the sweat off the cans before they twisted the beers from the plastic rings. They stood in their coats and drank without women.

An old man came walking slowly up the sidewalk with two fifths of bourbon in a paper bag. His knees were unbent and the snowy wind propelled him forward and he needed a cane though he did not use one. He made his way along by the curb slush until he stood beneath the awning. Len could see that he wore braces under his baggy overalls. The old man nodded a long minute before saying a word.

"Party's inside, son," he said. "It's bad luck to go to bed sober after burying a friend."

"I've never heard that."

"Sure. The pecker gnats will get you. There's about three sons of bitches I hope stay sober the day they plant me. Two of them are inside."

"And the other isn't cold in the ground yet," Len said.

The old man tilted up his hat brim. He smiled and shook his head.

"If you ain't Bruno Konick when he come back from overseas. You must be his boy."

"Yessir."

"Dilute Polack with hillbilly and it's the Polack that sticks," the old man said. "I'm sorry. We won't see another like him."

Len wanted to call him a liar, but instead looked through the window at the men eating baloney sandwiches and their empty beer cans on the tables. He nodded his thanks.

"You coming in?" the old man said.

"I don't think so."

"Beware of the pecker gnats."

The old man shook Len's hand and pushed open the door with his shoulder. The wind blew snow off the sidewalk and into the diner's foyer where the puddles were printed like boot soles. The men were laughing, their mouths to bottle necks, teeth goring chicken legs. The yellow light fell through the window, but illuminated nothing. Len walked off down the street.

He drove out Waldron Highway in the Chevy Caprice lent him by Art Bertrand and headed for Watega while the snow powdered the ditch ice and shifted like the turning of the desert sands. The town rose so suddenly from the fields with streetlights aglow and traffic making way for the foundries that he wondered what thought preoccupied him these fifteen miles. His mind was tired and he could not remember. He now knew that his thoughts and memories were of little consequence and the world went its own way and let men think that they took their own road. He felt the years of his journey like a useless sleep and wondered what might erase the traces. Perhaps some blue morning. Perhaps the dark from a cold starry night.

Court Street was empty in the snow and the early dusk except for the train cars making their way slowly across the viaduct. He found the old man's truck parked in front of the recruiting station. The bed was filled with snow and ashlogs but someone had cleared the ice off the windshield that morning. The old snow showed black beneath the fresh powder and it was heaped upon the curb by the plows so that the heads of the parking meters were buried. Len shut down the engine and watched the flakes disappear into the hood. He went inside. The salt was blue on the sidewalk, melting the ice without sun.

The sergeant sat behind his desk in a starched khaki shirt. A cigarette burned in an ashtray overflowing with butts. He sipped coffee from a mug that bore the stripes of his rank while two black kids sat on a vinyl couch and filled out forms attached to clipboards. They were tall boys and had big hands but their faces were small and gentle. The sergeant sat down his mug and Len studied the boys.

"Is it your wife you want to be shut of?" the sergeant said. "Or does she want your ass gone? If you can get two people to vouch you ain't pushing forty, I got a job for you."

Len looked at the sergeant and he smiled. In the office light, Len saw that his face was wrecked. His nose was crooked, his eyes were sunken, he had pocked cheeks. It was like raw chicken in color. The kids chewed the pens and pronounced words three times before writing them on the forms.

"I can't give you back your old rank, either," the sergeant said. "I'd be drunk for fifty years if I had a dime for every time I got asked that."

"I just want to know when Luke Konick left for boot camp," Len said. "We buried his grandpa today and he never showed."

"You his uncle?"

"Yes."

The sergeant drew his eyes. His jaw stuck out.

"Len Konick your name?" he asked.

"That's me."

The sergeant handed him the old man's keys over the desk, then sat back in the swivel chair with his cigarette. Len looked at the top of the ignition key worn by the old man's thumb and forefinger. He saw him leaned against a fence watching the rain fall on freshly cut fields. *I can love him if I only remember the small things.*

"I'm sorry about your father, sir," the sergeant said. "My job is only to get him on the bus."

Len nodded vaguely. The old man was gone, but the fence and the country remained.

"Now before you read me my rights for enlisting him," the sergeant said, "I got to tell you I was a Hue City marine. You ain't the first Vietnam veteran who ever showed up here asking me how I can do this. My answer is practical. Just go stand on the sidewalk and take a long look at this town and come back and tell me what the hell Watega, Illinois has for any of these boys. The union halls got waiting lists four years long and no college would take them."

"I'm not here for that," Len said. "I just want to know how I can get ahold of Luke Konick."

"That's easy," the sergeant said. "He's sitting at the bus station right now. The snow's got everything moved back three hours."

"Thank you."

"There ain't going to be no more Vietnams," the sergeant said. "I can swear it right now. These boys will be able to win. There won't be no good gook, bad gook shit with President Reagan. That man give us back something."

Len held the truck keys and nodded his thanks. *The small things.* He turned to leave, but turned back.

"My father won his war," Len said, "but looking at his life you wouldn't be able to tell it."

The sergeant's cigarette ash fell on his blue trousers. He watched it roll and crumble.

"How'd you know I was in Vietnam?" Len said.

"The draft was pretty thorough in towns like these," the sergeant said. "I come from one like it in Ohio."

"They didn't leave a rock unturned," Len said. "Not a god-damned one."

The sergeant did not watch him leave. The black kids were struggling with the spellings of the streets where they lived. Len listened while the boys sounded out the words slowly and discussed their findings amongst themselves as if each syllable contained a great mystery. Perhaps a riddle to trick them out of enlisting. Len stopped outside on the sidewalk. The snow was lining the hickories on the courthouse lawn where the statue of the Union soldier stood guard with a rifle and bayonet and many branches had broken from the weight of the snow.

* * *

In the Greyhound station an old man mopped the floor where the linoleum met the door and the mop head kept time with his whistling of big band music. One by one the black footprints vanished from the tile squares. The terminal shared the building with a garage and smelled of solvent and fresh oil and there were only four benches without backs and a pop machine Len saw the mechanics used because the buttons were filthy. Tickets were bought on the bus. He stood in the door while the old man straightened the floor mats with his boot heel. The wind blew snow inside and it disappeared into the clean floor. The old man closed the door without looking at him. The hearing aid fastened behind his earlobe squeaked and he wore dirty long-sleeved underwear.

"Come on," he said.

"I don't want to mess it up right after you finished," Len said.

"I'm here until ten o'clock. You can only stare so long out the window."

"It's got to be a pain never finishing."

The old man's legs hurt him and he leaned on the mop like a crutch. He scanned the tiles for footprints.

"A floor ain't meant to stay clean," he said, "just for me to clean it."

Luke sat alone in blue jeans and a shirt that looked as if he'd bought them new at JC Penny. The clothes held the creases the way the clerks had folded them for the display tables. His boots were propped on the bench before him and he smoked until he finished his Coke, then dropped the butt into the can. Len walked over and sat down beside him. The snowflakes melted when they hit the station windows. Luke pitched the can in the trash barrel and looked at the empty benches.

"I watched him die," he said. "I just want you to know that before you say shit. It's all the funeral I'll ever need."

"There wasn't much but old men with gravestones in their eyes," Len said.

191

"They were just hungover. Keeping company with drunks made him feel superior."

"He needed to think that," Len said.

"You're pretty forgiving. He told people you were dead."

"He needed to think that too."

They lit cigarettes and stared at the floor. The old man came from the restroom shaking his head and pushing a bucket of fresh water back toward the doorway. The wheels streaked the tiles and the steam rose through the strainer and up along the mop handle. Luke let the ash fall off his cigarette.

"He ever tell you about the war?" he said.

"No."

"Me either."

"I think he thought about it all the time," Len said.

"I know it. He could just go quiet on you for a long minute. His eyes got different. But you could never get him to talk about it. I don't think he even told Art Bertrand."

"He didn't have to. Art was in the Pacific."

Luke smoked and his hand trembled when he took the cigarette from his mouth. The enlistment papers sat beside him in a yellow envelope.

"I kept thinking it would be something big to watch him die," Luke said. "Like I could see life passing somewhere else and if I looked real hard I could see it happening. I'd know then that one thing was really true. But there was only that green line going flat. I wanted to see a dove in the window. Shit. Anything that would let me know you finally get the hell out of here."

Len looked at Luke and wiped his eyes.

"After he died," Luke said, "I walked off through the parking lot thinking about what them priests used to tell us about the day when all the bodies and the souls of dead people get joined together again. That's just shit. I don't think one of them ever saw two crows eating the guts out of a rabbit. What's my old man going to do? Walk around heaven without a face? It's all hard enough, but then they got to go lying to you. But you know what I really hate?"

"What?" Len had not answered right away.

"Ending up here on this bench."

"You haven't ended up anywhere yet."

"Shit," Luke said. "I've fallen right in line."

They sat quietly upon the benches and listened to the bus make its way up the street. Luke stared at his ticket and Len watched the snow blow under the door. The old man leaned against the wall and held the mop handle straight in the bucket where the steam had stopped rising. The wind rushed in every tree and piece of gutter metal and by the time the bus parked, they could not see it because the snow covered the windows. The old man opened the door and two passengers came inside followed by the wind and the blowing snow. They walked through the door to the garage, sexless in hats and heavy coats. He pointed at Luke, but never looked at him.

"I think that's you," Len said.

Luke put on his mackinaw and took up his bag and papers. He held the ticket ready for the driver to punch. Neither of his hands was free to shake.

"How you fixed for cigarettes?" Len asked.

"Got a carton in my bag," Luke said.

"You'll come back bad with the habit."

"I already got it bad."

"Well," Len said, "there were things I was going to tell you. But they were for a boy and you aren't a boy."

"You think so?" Luke said.

"A boy couldn't know what you know."

"I thought you was a freak son of a bitch when you first showed up," Luke said. "But that ain't true. I wasn't used to someone knowing what I was feeling."

"Fair enough," Len said.

"I just hope you found what you come back looking for," Luke said.

"I'll tell you about it one of these days."

"It ain't my business. I got enough to remember them by. Be good now, Uncle Len."

"Yeah. You be good."

Luke walked out the door and when the old man closed it, he leaned into the metal to make the latch snap against the wind. Len started for the window to watch the bus drive away but remembered they were all white. The old man moved the mop across the footprints and resumed whistling the old songs. Len stood a while among the empty benches, forcing feelings, but it wasn't any good. It was hard to feel anything after saying goodbye to strangers. He turned and left out of the side door and walked back through the snow to the car.

The snow became stray flakes and the black clouds lifted from the horizon and the sun shone dim and pale. Len drove the roads east from town that were cleared by the county salt trucks and hard black from contrasting with the white fields and the heaped snow the plowblades had pushed against the roadside. The snow quit altogether and white light broke sudden and pure from the west through torn clouds and he looked at the country which was more aglow in twilight than noon. The light glared through the black river trees in a way that made him believe sight became sound. Wind in rocks. Rain upon mountain tops. The falling of timber in high forests. He left the car in a snowbank and climbed out and walked knee deep down a field road for the river trees where the wind blew snow off the branches and swept the clouds across the sun until the overcast was gone.

The western horizon burned as if on fire. He made his way through the deadfall in the twilight. The sun etched stark shadows upon the snow, branches thinly woven, the trunks stretched long and gaunt. He headed for the glowing river and sat on a stump and wished the water would brighten enough to burn his eyes, but it darkened by slow degrees, and the shadows of the trees and himself blurred on the snow. In time his sight was only sight and not sound at all. He put his face into his hands and cried over the loss.

The wind was down and the woods seemed forever paused with drawn breath. *It will all pass. It will all flee.*

Before sunset he became very cold and looked up from his hands. Deer were making their way in pairs through the poled birches that grew along the ridge and sauntering down through the last of the tree shadows and the spotted young moved close beside the does. He felt the young buck looking at him with dark and burning eyes long before he turned his own eyes. Their stare fixed and Len saw the breath fuming from his nostrils. The herd did not change the way of their coming to the river. They had no fear of him at all. He thought himself deadfall to them, inanimate yet of the world. The deer passed down through a culvert where scrub trees twisted from the drifts. The light turned sallow and dissolved behind the ridge.

Len rose and walked into the scaled birches toward the coming deer. The young buck stood unmoved as a sentry and followed Len with glowing eyes while he printed over the buck's small tracks in the snow. The wind was gentle. He leaned against a ruined oak and raised his wet face and the herd passed so close to him that he felt the heat of their breath. They broke dry sticks beneath the snow. The yearlings wore spots white like the birches and the does were fat from field corn and the great bucks pushed away the low hanging branches with their antlers. The deer came down the little slope and went parallel with the river. Len stepped forward from the dead oak with his hands raised to greet them or confer a blessing upon the ground they trod. In time he walked off among them and trailed the herd with the young and the old, their breath mingling in the grainy light while the young buck loped ahead into the darkness hooding the woods. The deer let him be and he thought little of the oddness and he closed his eyes and walked through the snow as if he walked in sleep.

The summer he left for the army a black kid from Leesville became the first boy from the county to have an empty casket sent home from Vietnam. It was also the summer of white-hot days where the dust hazed the sun. The young corn burned in the furrow lines. The rains came too late and the squalls moved through the country with lightning that set the dry river trees ablaze and the rain steamed and hissed in the fires. That summer he fished the Watega for large-mouth bass and thought little of the black kid's name buried in the cemetery between the bottom fields and the river's south fork where heavyset matrons with wrapped heads watched his passing coldly from the porches of weathered shotgun houses. He did not know him and he told himself many times that he could not mourn when he did not love.

The last time he fished the Watega was the morning after a night of cold rains that made the darkness hold two temperatures. By dawn the storm had passed and the upturned trees lay charred and dead across the culverts and the sunlight seared the rain smell from the new light. He walked all morning upon the drying mud and headed east through the trees mauled by the storm. He carried a rod with tackle in a haversack slung across his shoulder, freeing a hand for the coffee can full of nightcrawlers.

It was noon when he found a shaded place to fish, a deep hole in the creek mouth with water dark from silt and last autumn's leaves. The old black was seated upon a folding chair. He had four teeth and hair like yellow snow and wore jeans covered with colored patches. Len knew him from the river. The man looked up from his cane pole and nodded his corrugated face, then lifted the line to check his stink bait. The smell made Len glance away where the sunlight strobed the woodvine.

"I told you about dipping your hook in shit," Len said.

The man pitched the line crosswise into the river and the current swept it back to where it was before. He nodded thoughtfully to himself. The line pulled taught in the white light.

"A storm confuses the fish real good," he said. "But not that good. No, youngblood. Nothing but a man will eat shit. This here's corn pone and spoiled milk."

The man's straw hat was black with sweat and he wiped his

cheeks with a ragged towel hanging from his neck and then pointed at a stringer of small bullheads flapping against the rocks. He grinned with his mouth closed.

"Damn, sir," Len said. "If it smells like shit, it must be shit."

"No fish will eat shit, youngblood. Not even a carp."

"My dad said he once found a man's finger in the belly of a carp," Len said.

"A finger ain't shit."

"Not unless the newspaper rips," Len said.

The old man was nodding his head.

"You sure sure of yourself, youngblood," he said. "You either going to end up dead or be the president. You read like tea leaves."

"I thought tea leaves were supposed to tell you for sure," Len said.

"Tea leaves only tell you if you going to be a thinking man or not. That's all."

Len walked over to see the bullheads strung through the gills and thrashing their tails.

"Mind if I fish here?" he asked.

"Not if you don't mind catching a piranha," the man said.

"There's no kind of fish like that here. It gets too cold."

"Anything can be anywhere, youngblood. Anytime. Any damned day."

"Maybe in South America," Len said.

"I caught me one here yesterday. He fought harder than two motherfuckers against the preacher on Easter Sunday. I could have used your legs."

"Did you take him off the hook?" Len said.

"No, sir. I threw the pole right into the river when I saw what I had. Life taught me a long time ago to leave be anything that's got more teeth than me."

Also from
AKASHIC BOOKS

Water in Darkness by Daniel Buckman
193 pages, hardcover
ISBN: 1-888451-19-X
AKB13 - $21.00

"Simply put, *Water in Darkness* is a superb novel . . . an earthbound 'Chicago' style that harkens back to *Studs Lonigan*, and reminds one of the close-to-the-bone, walk-the-plank stories of Mike Royko, Stuart Dybek, and Nelson Algren. Buckman speaks for a new, young generation of soldiers who thought they were at peace . . . the best new fiction I have read in a good long while."
—Larry Heinemann, author of *Paco's Story*, winner of the National Book Award

Heart of the Old Country by Tim McLoughlin
Selected for the Barnes & Noble Discover Great New Writers Program

216 pages, trade paperback
ISBN: 1-888451-15-7
AKB11 - $14.95

"Tim McLoughlin writes about South Brooklyn with a fidelity to people and place reminiscent of James T. Farrell's *Studs Lonigan* and George Orwell's *Down and Out in Paris and London* . . . No voice in this symphony of a novel is more impressive than that of Mr. McLoughlin, a young writer with a rare gift for realism and empathy."
—Sidney Offit, author of *Memoir of the Bookie's Son*

The Snow Train by Joseph Cummins
290 pages, trade paperback
ISBN: 1-888451-23-8
AKB17 - $14.95

"A groundbreaking first novel that tackles nothing less daunting than the fragile psyche of early childhood."
—Kaylie Jones, author of *A Soldier's Daughter Never Cries*

"An intriguing worldview, meticulously assembled with an artist's inspired touch." —*Kirkus Reviews*

Adios Muchachos by Daniel Chavarría
Nominated for a 2001 Edgar Award!

245 pages, paperback
ISBN: 1-888451-16-5
AKB12 - $13.95

A selection in the Akashic Cuban Noir series. ". . . [A] zesty Cuban paella of a novel that's impossible to put down. This is a great read . . ." —*Library Journal*

Jerusalem Calling by Joel Schalit
218 pages, trade paperback
ISBN: 1-888451-17-3
AKB20 - $14.95

"This remarkable collection of essays by an astute young writer covers a wide range of topics—the political ethic of punk, the nature of secular Jewish identity, the dangerous place, according to Schalit, that politicized Christianity plays in the U.S., and the legacy of the Cold War in the ability to imagine freedom. Schalit almost always hits his mark . . . This is the debut of a new and original thinker." —*Publishers Weekly* (starred review)

Spy's Fate by Arnaldo Correa
305 pages, hardcover
ISBN: 1-888451-28-9
AKB26 - $24.95

"Arnaldo Correa gives us a courageous book that offers a true insider's view of the new Cuba: the Cuba that has emerged since the fall of the Soviet Union; the Cuba that neither the United States government nor Fidel Castro wants you to know about." —William Heffernan, Edgar Award-winning author of *Red Angel*

Synthetic Bi Products by Sparrow L. Patterson
341 pages, trade paperback
ISBN: 1-888451-18-1
AKB16 - $15.95

Sparrow L. Patterson's debut novel follows a nineteen-year-old bisexual girl on her whirlwind journey of sexual escapades, drug-induced hallucinations, shoplifting sprees, and other criminal behavior. Sexy and romantic, a fast-paced story of lust, deception, and heartache, *Synthetic Bi Products* is a compelling and original novel narrated in a bold, fresh, funny voice.

These books are available at local bookstores.
They can also be purchased with a credit card online through www.akashicbooks.com.

To order by mail, send a check or money order to:
Akashic Books
PO Box 1456
New York, NY 10009

Prices include shipping. Outside the U.S., add $3 to each book ordered.